Love's Long Journey

Books by Janette Oke

www.janetteoke.com

Another Homecoming* • Return to Harmony*
Tomorrow's Dream*

ACTS OF FAITH*

The Centurion's Wife   The Hidden Flame
The Damascus Way

CANADIAN WEST

When Calls the Heart   When Breaks the Dawn
When Comes the Spring   When Hope Springs New

Beyond the Gathering Storm
When Tomorrow Comes

LOVE COMES SOFTLY

Love Comes Softly   Love's Unending Legacy
Love's Enduring Promise   Love's Unfolding Dream
Love's Long Journey   Love Takes Wing
Love's Abiding Joy   Love Finds a Home

A PRAIRIE LEGACY

The Tender Years   A Quiet Strength
A Searching Heart   Like Gold Refined

SEASONS OF THE HEART

Once Upon a Summer   Winter Is Not Forever
The Winds of Autumn   Spring's Gentle Promise

SONG OF ACADIA*

The Meeting Place   The Birthright
The Sacred Shore   The Distant Beacon
The Beloved Land

WOMEN OF THE WEST

The Calling of Emily Evans   A Bride for Donnigan
Julia's Last Hope   Heart of the Wilderness
Roses for Mama   Too Long a Stranger
A Woman Named Damaris   The Bluebird and the Sparrow
They Called Her Mrs. Doc   A Gown of Spanish Lace
The Measure of a Heart   Drums of Change

*with Davis Bunn

JANETTE OKE

Love's Long Journey

BETHANY HOUSE
MINNEAPOLIS, MINNESOTA

Love's Long Journey
Copyright © 1982, 2003
Janette Oke

Newly edited and revised

Cover design by Jennifer Parker
Cover model photography by Jason Jorgensen

Published by Bethany House Publishers
11400 Hampshire Avenue South
Bloomington, Minnesota 55438

Bethany House Publishers is a division of
Baker Publishing Group, Grand Rapids, Michigan.

Printed in the United States of America

ISBN   978-0-7642-2850-6

Library of Congress Cataloging-in-Publication Data

Oke, Janette, 1935–
    Love's long journey / by Janette Oke.
        p.   cm. — (Love comes softly ; bk. 3)
    ISBN 0-7642-2850-1
    1. Davis family (Fictitious characters : Oke)—Fiction.   2. Women pioneers—Fiction.
I. Title.   II. Series: Oke, Janette, 1935-   . Love comes softly series ; bk. 3.
    PR9199.3.O38L6   2003
    813'.54—dc21   2003014742

This book is dedicated to you,

the readers of *Love Comes Softly*

and *Love's Enduring Promise,*

with thanks for your kind words

of encouragement.

JANETTE OKE was born in Champion, Alberta, to a Canadian prairie farmer and his wife, and she grew up in a large family full of laughter and love. She is a graduate of Mountain View Bible College in Alberta, where she met her husband, Edward, and they were married in May of 1957. After pastoring churches in Indiana and Canada, the Okes spent some years in Didsbury and Calgary, where Edward served in several positions on college faculties while Janette continued her writing. She has written over five dozen novels for adults and children, and her book sales total over twenty-two million copies.

The Okes have three sons and one daughter, all married, and are enjoying their dozen grandchildren. Edward and Janette are active in their local church and make their home near Didsbury, Alberta.

Visit Janette Oke's Web site at: *www.janetteoke.com*.

Contents

Prologue

Let's imagine for a moment a family separation back in the days of the pioneers. Grown children have announced to their parents that the West is calling them.

For weeks and months the entire family is in a fever-pitch of excitement and activity, making plans, sewing clothing and bedding, purchasing and packing crates and crocks with supplies sufficient for many months—or even years. All the food, from coffee to flour, lard to honey, molasses to salt—and other items pickled, salted, dried, canned—is collected and prepared for the long journey. Lamps and fuel are needed, grease for the wagons, repair parts for the harnesses, as well as guns and gunpowder, tools, nails, rope, crocks, kettles, pots and pans, dishes, medicines, seeds, and material to make more clothing when what they wore would become threadbare. Any furniture or equipment that the family can afford and find room for is packed in the wagons—stove, sewing machine, bed, table, and chairs all have to be taken along.

Breakables are carefully packed in sawdust and crated in handmade boxes. Everything needs to be protected against possible water damage, for there will be rivers to ford and rains to endure. At the journey's end, the crates will be unpacked and disassembled, every board hoarded for some future building project—a window frame, a stool, a baby's crib. The sawdust will be sparingly used to feed a fire, sprinkled lightly over smoking buffalo chips.

The crocks and jars containing food will be used for other storage when their original purpose is complete.

Yes, it is a monumental task. The preparation for such a move will tax minds, bodies, and emotions to the limit. But when the sorting and packing is finished, the wagons are loaded and the teams hitched and ready to move out—what then?

Mothers and fathers will bid their offspring farewell with the knowledge they might be seeing them for the last time. Communication by letter across country will take many months, if such letters arrive at all. So parents in the East will know next to nothing of their children's and grandchildren's whereabouts or their well-being. Those who stay behind no doubt hope that no news is good news—for only bad news is of sufficient import to be delivered across the empty miles.

Wife follows husband, convinced that her rightful place is by his side regardless of the strong tug toward the home she has known and loved. Danger, loneliness, and possible disaster await them in the new world toward which they are heading, but she goes nonetheless.

I often think about those pioneer women. What it must have cost many of them to follow their husband's dream! To venture forth, leaving behind the things that represented safety and security; to birth their babies unattended; to nurse sick children with no medicines or doctors; to be mother, teacher, minister, physician, tailor, and grocer to a growing family; to support their men without complaint through floods, blizzards, sandstorms, and droughts; to walk tall when there was little to wear, little to work with, and even less to eat.

God bless them all—the women who courageously went forth with their men. And bless those who stood with tear-filled eyes and aching hearts and let their loved ones go. And grant to us a measure of the faith, strength, courage, love, and determination that prompted them to do what they did.

Janette Oke

ONE

The Journey Begins

Missie experimentally pushed back her bonnet and let the rays of the afternoon sun fall directly on her head. She wasn't sure if that was preferable, since the loss of protection from the sun with the shade from its wide brim also kept the slight breeze from her face. It certainly was hot! She comforted herself with the thought that the worst of the day's heat was already past—surely it would begin to cool before long as the sun moved lower in the western sky.

Her first day on the trail seemed extremely long and tiring. The excitement of the morning's early departure already felt as if it were weeks behind her. But no, time insisted it truly had been only at the dawning of this very day when they had exchanged painful good-byes with her beloved family.

As she recalled the tears and sadness of the morning, Missie also felt a tingle of excitement go through her. She and Willie were really heading west! After all the planning and dreaming, they were actually on the way. From her perch on the seat at the front of the wagon, the dream, though still a long way off, was now anchored in reality.

Missie's weary, aching body verified that they were indeed on the way, and she shifted on the hard wooden boards to try for a more comfortable position. Willie turned to her, though she knew his hands expertly holding the reins were still aware of every movement of the plodding team.

"Ya tirin'?" he asked. His eyes searched her hot face.

Missie smiled in spite of her distress and pushed back some strands of damp hair. "A bit. About time for me to stretch my legs again, I reckon."

Willie nodded and turned back to the horses he was driving. "I miss ya when yer not here beside me," he told her, "but I sure won't deny ya none any relief ya might be gettin' from a walk now an' then. Ya wantin' down now?"

"In a few minutes." Missie fell silent, then commented, "Sure's one bustling, dusty way to travel, this going by wagon train." She could feel Willie's sideways glance at her as she continued, "Harness creaking, horses stomping, people shouting—hadn't realized it would be so noisy."

"I 'spect it'll quieten some as we all get used to it." Willie's tone sounded a bit anxious.

"Yeah, I reckon so," Missie assured him quickly. He had enough to worry about without wondering if she was all right.

She reached out to tuck a hand under Willie's arm. She could feel his muscles tighten as he pulled her hand against his body in silent communication. She could see the strength in his arms as they gave firm guidance to the team. His coarse cotton shirt was damp in many places, and Missie noticed he had undone a couple of buttons at the neck.

"Guess we just brought our noise and bustle along with us," she said wryly.

"Meanin'?"

"Well, you know what it's been like at home for all these weeks we've been planning, packing, crating, loading—it seemed it would never end. And the noise was really something—everybody talking at once, hammers pounding, and barrels and pans banging. It was like a madhouse, that's what it was."

Willie laughed. "Was kinda, wasn't it?"

Silence again.

Missie could feel Willie steal a glance her way. She made no further comment, and finally Willie spoke cautiously. "Ya seem to be thinkin' awful deep like."

Missie allowed a quiet sigh to escape from her lips and tightened her grip on Willie's arm. "Not deep . . . just thinking of home. It must seem awfully quiet there now. Awfully quiet. After all the days and months of getting ready. . . ." Missie was so taken up with her reverie she didn't finish her sentence, and Willie did not interrupt.

Missie thought of their two wagons crammed full. Never had she dreamed it possible to get so much into two wagons. Everything they would be needing in the months ahead had been loaded into those wagons—and a fair number of things they could very well have lived without if they'd had to, Missie realized with some chagrin. She thought particularly of the fancy dishes her ma had purchased with some of her own egg money and insisted on packing in sawdust herself. "Someday you'll be glad thet ya made the room," Marty had assured her. And Missie knew in her heart that she would indeed look at the dishes with the bittersweet joy and memories they brought to her soul.

A sense of sadness overtook her, and she had no desire to have Willie read her mind. The thoughts of home and loved ones brought a sharp pain deep inside of her. If she weren't careful, she'd be in tears. She swallowed hard and forced a smile as she turned to him.

"Maybe I should get in a little more walking now," she said briskly.

"I'll pull over right up there ahead at thet widenin' in the road," he promised.

Missie nodded.

"Have you noticed we're already beyond the farms we know?" Willie asked.

"I've noticed."

"Makes it seem more real. Like we really are goin' west." The genuine jubilance in his voice made her smile. She did share his joy and excitement, but at the same instant that now-familiar pain twisted within her. She was going west with Willie—but she was leaving behind all the others she knew and loved. When would she see them again? *Would* she see them again . . . ever? Tears pressed against her eyes.

Willie pulled the team over for a quick stop so she could climb down over the wagon wheel. The dust whirled up as he moved on without her, and Missie stepped away a few paces and turned her back. She pulled her bonnet up to keep the dust from settling on her hair. She waited until both their wagons had passed, giving a brief nod to the young fellow they had hired to drive their second team, then looked around for someone she might have already met among the other walkers who followed the teams. She didn't recognize anyone right off, so Missie smiled at those closest to her and, without a word, took a position in that group.

As she walked the dusty, rutted road, her body, though young and healthy, hurt all over. She wondered how the older women were able to keep going. She glanced about her at two women walking slightly to her right. *They look 'bout Ma's age,* she mused. *She is well and strong and can often outwork me. But, still, I wouldn't want to see her have to put in such a day.*

The women did look tired, and Missie's heart went out to them. Then she remembered the wagon master, Mr. Blake, giving the whole group their instructions that morning. At the time it had seemed foolish to Missie to even consider having a short day the first few days on the trail. Now she understood the wisdom in Mr. Blake's announcement. The sun was

gradually moving toward the horizon, and they would be stopping soon, she was sure. She moved over to the two ladies and
introduced herself. A bit of a chat would help them all get their
minds off their aching bodies.

When their conversation had tapered off, Missie's thoughts
turned to Willie. She wondered if he would welcome the early
camp tonight, or if his eagerness to reach their destination
would make him want to push on.

Missie was proud of Willie, proud of his good looks. He
had a dark head of slightly curling hair, deep brown eyes, a
strong chin with an indentation akin to a dimple (though
Willie would never allow her to call it such), a well-shaped
nose that had narrowly spared perfection by his fall from a tree
when he was nine years old—these descriptions were her Willie. So were the broad shoulders, the tall frame, the strong arms.

But when Missie thought of Willie, she pictured not only
the man whom others saw but his character she had come to
know so well. Willie, who was as manly as any but who seemed
to read her thoughts, who considered others first, who was
flexible when dealing with others but steadfast when dealing
with himself. This was a man who was strong and purposeful
in his decisions—a mite stubborn, some felt, but Missie preferred to describe him as having "strength of determination."
Well, maybe a *little* stubborn, she conceded, if being stubborn
was hanging on to a dream—his dream of raising cattle, of
working with fine horses, of owning his own ranch, of going
further west.

When Willie, two years previously, had made the trip west
to seek out the spread of his dreams, he had persevered through
seemingly endless searching and red tape until he actually held
in his hand the title deed for the land. After he and Missie were
married and when their actual going had been delayed in order
to set aside the money needed for the venture, Willie had

chafed at the delay, but his dream had not died. He had worked hard at the mill, laying aside every penny they could spare until he felt sure they had saved enough. Missie had been proud to add whatever she could from her teacher's salary to make the sum grow more quickly. It gave her a sense of having a part in Willie's dream. It was now becoming her dream, too.

Missie's glance lifted to the sky to figure out the time by the sun. She calculated it was somewhere between three and four o'clock.

Back home the time of day was easily distinguished by the activity in evidence. Right now her ma would be taking a break from heavier tasks, spending some time in her favorite chair with mending or knitting. Her pa would still be in the field. They, too, had been awfully generous in adding to Willie's little nest egg. She then thought of the final moments with her parents. Though it had happened just this morning, time and distance were no longer the only measurements. That was her other life, and she was now heading to a new life, the one she had chosen with Willie.

Pa and Ma had been so brave as they had bid her good-bye. Clark had gathered them all close around him and led them in family prayer. Marty had tried desperately not to cry. At Missie's "It's all right, Mama . . . go ahead and cry if you want to," the tears did come—for both of them. The two held each other close and wept, and afterward Missie could tell her ma felt a similar measure of relief and comfort as she did.

Missie now brushed away unbidden tears and glanced about to see if she had been observed. Deliberately she pushed the thoughts of loneliness from her. If she weren't careful, she'd work herself into a real state and arrive in camp with red-rimmed eyes and blotchy cheeks. Besides, she had Willie—she need never be *truly* lonesome. And her pa's prayer that morning was a reminder that "the Lord was goin' a'fore and behind" them on their way.

Missie trudged on, placing one tired foot before the other. Even in sturdy walking shoes, her feet looked small, and she knew the plain brown cotton frock did not hide her youthfulness. She had overheard two fellow travelers commenting on "thet wisp of a thing ain't gonna last a week—why, she can't possibly be more'n fifteen!" She couldn't decide whether to laugh or cry about the whole exchange, so she decided to do neither. They probably wouldn't believe she had a normal-school teaching certificate and two years of teaching behind her. But she certainly intended to prove them wrong and pull her weight with the rest of this little traveling community.

Missie now raised a hand to push away some hair that had come untucked and insisted upon wisping about her face. Strands of it clung to the dampness of her moist forehead. She knew her normally fair cheeks were flushed from the heat of the day. In spite of homesickness, weariness, and the hot sun overhead, she couldn't help feeling Willie's enthusiasm and excitement as she looked forward to their new life in their own place.

Missie's attention was drawn back to her traveling companions. Some of the women were now gathering dry sticks and twigs as they followed the wagons. A number of children also were running here and there, picking up suitable fuel, as well. *They must be anticipating stopping soon,* Missie thought, so she, too, began to look about as she walked, gathering fuel for her own fire.

A commotion ahead brought Missie's attention back to the wagons. The drivers were breaking line and maneuvering into a circle as they had been instructed that morning. Missie's steps quickened. It wouldn't be long now until she would be resting in some shade. How wonderful it would be just to sit down for a spell and let the afternoon breeze cool her warm face and body! She was looking forward, also, to chatting with Willie and learning how he had fared in the short time they had been apart.

Missie wondered, with a fluttering of her pulse, if tonight by their campfire would be the time to whisper to Willie about her growing conviction that *perhaps* they were to become parents. She was quite sure now, though she still had not mentioned it to him. *Don't want to raise false hopes—or cause concern for no reason,* she had told herself.

Would Willie be pleased? She knew how he loved youngsters, and she knew his eagerness to have a son of his own. But she could also guess his concern for her in their current circumstances. He had hoped to make the trip west and be settled in their own home *before* starting a family. A long wagon trip could be very difficult for an expectant mother. Yes, Willie might just feel the baby could have selected a more appropriate and convenient time.

Missie had no such misgivings. She was young and healthy, and besides, they would reach Willie's land long before the baby was due. Still, she had to admit to herself that she had put off telling Willie her suspicions until they were actually on the trail. She had been somewhat anxious that if he knew, he would suggest postponing their journey until after the birth, and to Missie's thinking, he had experienced enough delay already.

So she had kept her precious secret. She hadn't dared even share it with her mother, though her whole being ached to do so. *She'll fret,* Missie had told herself. *She'll never rest easy for one night while we're on the trail.*

In the distance Missie spotted their wagons side by side in the big circle. Willie was unhitching the team from their first wagon, and Henry Klein, their hired driver, was working with the second team. When they had begun to load weeks before, it became evident one wagon was not going to be sufficient to provide both living quarters on the way plus transportation for all their supplies and household needs. Missie's father, Clark, had suggested the second wagon and had even helped in locating a driver. Many other members of the wagon train also had more than one wagon, but most of them were fortunate enough to have another family member who could drive the teams. Willie wouldn't have considered for one minute Missie's serving in such a capacity.

As Missie neared their wagons, the twenty-seventh one creaked into position, the driver sweating and shouting to his horses as they completed the circle for the train's overnight stop.

Missie approached Willie now and responded to his grin with a smile of her own.

"Been a long day. Yer lookin' tired," he said, concern in his eyes.

"I am a bit. The sun's been so hot it sure takes the starch out of me."

"It's time fer a good rest. Bit of that shade should revive ya some. Ya wantin' me to bring ya a stool or a blanket from the wagon to sit on?"

"I'll do it. You have the team to care for."

"Mr. Blake says there's a stream jest beyond thet stand of timber there. We're gonna take all the stock down fer a drink an' then tether them in the draw. Blake says there's plenty a' grass there."

"What time are you wanting supper?" Missie asked.

"Not fer a couple hours anyway. Ya got lotsa time fer a rest."

"I'll need more firewood. I didn't start gathering soon enough. That little bit I brought in won't last any time."

"No rush fer a fire, either. I'll bring some wood back with me. Henry won't mind bringin' some, too. Ya jest git a little time outta thet hot sun fer a while—ya look awfully tuckered out." Willie's voice continued to sound anxious.

"It's just the excitement and strangeness of it all, I expect. I'll get used to it. But right now I think I'll take a bit of rest in the shade of those trees. I'll be as good as new when I can get off my feet some."

Willie left with the horses and the two milk cows that had been tied behind the wagons. Missie went for a blanket to place on the ground in the shade of the trees.

She felt a bit guilty as she lowered herself onto the blanket. All the other women were busy with something. Well, she'd just rest a short while and then she would begin their supper preparations, as well. For the moment it felt good just to sit.

Missie leaned back comfortably against the trunk of a tree and closed her eyes, turning her head slightly so she could take full advantage of the gentle breeze. It teased at the loose strands of her hair and fanned her flushed face. All her bones cried out for a warm, relaxing soak in a tub. If she were home . . . but Missie quickly put that thought away from her. Her folks' big white house with its homey kitchen and wide stairway was no longer *her* home. The upstairs room with its cheerful rugs and frilly curtains was no longer *her* room. She was totally Willie's responsibility now, and Willie was hers. She prayed a short prayer that she would be worthy of such a man as her Willie— that God would help her make a home for him filled with happiness and love. And then, her eyes still closed, she felt the achiness weighing her whole body down on the blanket.

Ignore it, she commanded herself. *Ignore it, and it will go away.*

TWO

Day's End

When Missie opened her eyes again, she was surprised at the changes that had taken place around her. It was much cooler now, and the sun that had shone down with such intense heat during the day was hanging, friendly and placid, low in the western sky.

The smell of woodsmoke was heavy in the air—a sharp, pleasant smell—and the odors of cooking food and boiling coffee made her insides twinge with hunger. Now fully awake, she looked around in embarrassment at the supper preparations. Surely every woman in the whole train had been busy and about while she slept. What must they think of her? Willie would soon be back from caring for the animals and not even find a fire started!

Missie hurried toward her wagons, swishing out her skirts and smoothing back her hair.

It took a moment for her to realize that the fire that burned directly in front of their wagons was *her* fire, and that the delicious smell of stew and coffee came from *her* own cooking pots. She was trying to sort it all out when Willie poked his head out of the wagon. His face still showed concern when he looked at her but changed quickly to an expression of relief. "Yer lookin' better. How ya feelin'?"

Missie stammered some, "I'm fine . . . truly, just fine."

Then she added in a lowered voice, "But shamed nigh to death."

"Shamed?" Willie's voice sounded unnecessarily loud to Missie. " 'Bout what?"

"Well . . . me sitting there sleeping in the middle of the day, and you . . . you making the fire, and the coffee and . . . my goodness, what must they all think of me . . . that my husband has to do his work and mine, too?"

"Iffen thet's all thet's troublin' ya," Willie responded, "I reckon we can learn to live with it. 'Sides, I didn't make the fire. Henry did. He was mighty anxious fer his supper. Boy, can thet fella eat! We're liable to have to butcher both of those cows jest to feed 'im, long before we reach where we're goin'."

"Henry's eaten?"

"Sure has. I think he even left us a little bit. Seemed in a big hurry to be off. There jest happens to be a couple a' young girls travelin' with this train. Think maybe Henry went to get acquainted like." Willie winked.

"Aren't you coming out?" Missie asked when Willie made no move to leave the wagon.

"I'm lookin' fer the bread. Can't find a thing in all these crocks, cans, an' boxes. Where'd ya put it, anyway? Henry wolfed down his food without it, but I'd sorta like a bit of bread to go with my supper."

Missie laughed. "Really!" she said, shaking her head, "Bet you almost took a bite of it. It's right there, practically under your nose." She clambered into the wagon. "Here, let me get it. Mama sent some of her special tarts for our first night out, too."

As Missie lifted the bread and tarts from the crock in which they had been stored, another tug pulled at her from somewhere deep inside. She could envision Marty's flushed face as she bent over her oven, removing the special baking for the young couple she loved so dearly.

Willie seemed to sense Missie's mood; his arms went round her and he pulled her close. "She'll be missin' you, too, long 'bout now," he said softly against her hair.

Missie swallowed hard. "I reckon she will," she whispered.

"Missie?" Willie hesitated. "Are ya sure? It's still not too late to turn back, ya know. Iffen yer in doubt. . . ? Iffen ya feel—"

"My goodness, no," Missie said emphatically. "There's not a doubt in my mind at all. I'm looking forward to seeing your land and building a home. You know that! Sure, I'll miss Mama and Pa and the family—'especially at first. But I just have to grow up, that's all. Everyone has to grow up *sometime*." How could Willie think she was so selfish as to deny him his dream?

"Yer sure?"

"I'm sure."

"It won't be an easy trip—you know thet."

"I know."

"An' it won't be easy even after we git there. There's no house yet, no neighbors, no church. You'll miss it all, Missie."

"I'll have you."

Willie pulled her back into his arms. "I'm afraid I'm not much to make up fer all thet you're losin'. But I love ya, Missie—I love ya so much."

"Then that's all I need," whispered Missie. "Love is the one thing I reckon I just couldn't do without, so—"she reached up and kissed him on his chin—"as long as you love me, I should make out just fine."

Missie drew back gently from Willie's arms. "We'd better be eating that supper you cooked. I'm powerful hungry."

Willie nodded. "But you might change yer mind once you've tasted my cookin'." They both laughed.

After they had finished their meal together and Missie had washed up the few dishes, Willie brought out their Bible. It was carefully wrapped in oiled paper with an inner wrap of soft doeskin.

"Been thinkin'," he said. "Our mornin's are goin' to be short and rushed. It might be easier fer us to have our readin' time at night."

Missie nodded and settled down beside him. It was still light enough to see, but the light would not last for long. Willie found his place and began in an even voice.

"Fear thou not; for I am with thee: be not dismayed; for I am thy God: I will strengthen thee; yea, I will help thee; yea, I will uphold thee with the right hand of my righteousness."[1]

He closed the Bible slowly.

"Yer pa underlined thet for us. When he handed me the Bible this morning, he read it to me and marked it with this red ribbon. He said fer us to claim thet verse fer our own and to read it every day, if need be, until we felt it real and meaningful in our hearts."

"It's a good verse," Missie said, her voice tremulous. If she closed her eyes, she was sure she would be able to see her pa sitting at the kitchen table with the family Bible open before him and all of the family gathered round. She could even hear his voice as he led them in the morning prayer time. Her pa—the spiritual leader of the home. No . . . not anymore. Willie was the head of her home now; he was her spiritual leader. Now she would look to him for strength and direction to get her through each day—whether happy or difficult. She was not Clark's little girl anymore; she was a woman—a woman and a wife. Clark had handed her into the care and keeping of Willie. And though Missie was sure that her father's love and prayers would always reach out to her, she also knew Clark was content in his knowledge that she had taken her rightful place in life . . . by Willie's side.

---

[1] Isaiah 41:10, KJV.

Missie reached for Willie's hand and clung to it as they prayed together. Willie thanked God for being with them through the day and for the love of those left behind. He prayed for God to comfort their hearts at this difficult time as he and Missie learned to live without their families near. He asked for safety as they traveled and for special strength for Missie in the long days ahead, his voice tight again with concern. Missie determined that tonight was not the time to share her secret. There was no need to trouble Willie. She'd wait until she had gotten used to the bumping and the walking and had toughened to the pace of the trail. Besides, she told herself, there was still a chance she could be wrong.

If she was right—and deep down inside, Missie admitted that indeed she must be—she was bound to gain new vigor and strength with each passing day. In fact, the fresh air and exercise would be good for her. She'd wait. She'd wait until Willie could see for himself that she was healthy and strong and then she'd tell her secret. Then he would be as excited over the coming event as she was.

Oh, if only she could have told her ma and pa. She would have looked into their faces and exclaimed with joy, "I think you're going to be Grandma and you Grandpa—now, what do you think of that?" They would have hugged and laughed and cried together in one grand tangle of happiness. It would have been so much fun to announce her good news. But that wasn't to be . . . and it wasn't the right time to announce it to Willie, either. She'd wait.

THREE

Another Day

Missie stirred herself with difficulty, testing her back, legs, and arms to see just how much pain the movement brought to her. How she ached! Her mind scrambled around for the reason. As sleep left her, it all came back, a mixture of excitement and misgivings. Willie and she were on the trail. They were headed west, and she had been jostled until she could stand it no more and then had walked behind the wagons until her body protested with every step. And now, after sleeping on the hard, confining bed in their new living quarters, she ached even more.

Willie must hurt, too, she thought. She reached for him, but her hand touched only his empty pillow. Willie had already quietly left the cramped canvas-covered wagon that was to be their home for many weeks.

Missie quickly pulled herself from her bed, suppressing a groan as she did so. "I suppose I've gone and done it again," she muttered. "Willie likely had to cook his own breakfast, too."

But after Missie quickly dressed and climbed stiffly down from the wagon, she was relieved to find the sun just casting its first rays of golden light over the eastern horizon. Very few people were stirring about the camp. Willie had started a fire and left it burning for her. Missie added a few more sticks and watched as the flames accepted them with crackling eagerness.

"Land sakes!" Missie exclaimed under her breath. "I wonder if I'll ever get my tied-up muscles all unwound." She began to pace back and forth, flinging and flexing her arms to limber them up. *Me, a farm girl, and so pampered that one good day's walking bothers me! Guess Mama didn't work me hard enough.* She shook her head ruefully.

As Missie stepped briskly back and forth she came across another good reason for keeping on the move. In the coolness of the morning, the mosquitoes were out in droves, and they all seemed to be hungry. After a quick visit to the nearby woods, Missie decided to return to the wagon for a long-sleeved sweater to protect her arms.

She poured a generous amount of river water from the bucket into the washbasin sitting on the shelf outside the wagon and began her morning wash. The water was cold, and Missie was relieved to reach for a rough towel to rub the warmth back into her face and hands. But she did feel refreshed and ready to begin her day. She draped the towel over its peg and started the breakfast preparations. The coffee was bubbling and the bacon and eggs sending out their early-morning "all's well" signals when their driver, Henry, made his appearance.

Missie thought of Henry as no more than a boy but smiled to herself as she realized he was at least as old as her Willie. *Still,* she thought, *he doesn't have the same grown-up manner Willie has.*

"Mornin', Henry."

"Mornin', ma'am."

The "ma'am" brought another smile to Missie's lips.

"Hungry?"

Henry grinned. "Sure am."

"Did you sleep well?"

"Pesky mosquitoes don't let nothin' sleep. Bet the horses had to swish and stomp all night."

"The mosquitoes didn't bother me until I got up this morning. Maybe we didn't have any in our wagon."

"Willie said they were botherin' him."

Missie looked up from turning the bacon. "That so? I guess I was just sleeping too soundly to notice. Do you know where he is?"

"We checked out the horses and the cows, an' then he went over to have a chat with Mr. Blake."

"Everything all right?" Her brow furrowed as she looked up from the frying pan.

"Right as rain. Willie jest wanted to chat a spell, I reckon— to see how far we're goin' today."

"Oh." Missie didn't have to worry. She began to set out the tin plates for the morning meal.

It wasn't long before she heard Willie's familiar whistle. Her heart gave its usual flutter. She loved to hear that tuneful sound. It was a sure sign that her world was all in proper order. Willie rounded the wagon and his whistling stopped.

"Well, I'll be. Ya sure are up bright an' early this mornin'," he joked. "Thought maybe Henry an' me . . ." But he stopped after a look at Missie's expression. "Mosquitoes drive ya out?"

Missie smiled. "Truth is, I didn't even notice them. My aching joints were the first to tell me it was time to do a little stretching. Are you feeling a bit stiff, too?"

"Reckon I'd be fibbin' iffen I didn't own up to feelin' a little sore here an' there," Willie said with a grin. "An' thet's all yer gonna git me to confess. Full-grown able-bodied man shouldn't be admittin' to even thet. Folks will be thinkin' I never worked a day in my life."

Missie glanced at her husband's well-muscled body. "If they do," she said, "they sure have got their eyes in the wrong place."

"Boy, do I ever hurt," Henry put in. "Never realized how sore one's arms could git from drivin' horses or how much work it is to just sit on thet bumpin' ole wagon seat."

"We'll git used to it," Willie assured him, rolling a log over to sit on it. "In a few days' time, we'll wonder why we ever felt it in the first place."

Willie asked God's blessing on the food and on the day ahead, then Missie served up their breakfast.

After they had eaten, Henry left to check the other wagon. As Missie washed up and packed away their supplies, Willie carefully inspected his wagon and harness. The others in the train were also moving about now. Amid the sounds of running and yelling children, barking dogs, and calling mothers, Missie heard a baby cry.

"Didn't know we had a baby along," she commented, watching Willie out of the corner of her eye.

"It's the Collins'," Willie answered. "Only 'bout seven months old, the father tol' me."

"Quite a venture for one so young."

"An' fer her young mama."

"This is her first?"

"No. She's got another one, too. Jest past two, I'm thinkin'."

Missie paused for a moment, then said, "She'll have her hands full. Maybe the rest of us women can give her a hand now and then."

"I'm sure she'd 'preciate thet," Willie said. "There's another woman with the train who might need a hand now an' then, as well."

Missie turned to face him. "Someone not well?"

"Oh, I hope she's well enough—not fer me to know or say—but she's expectin' a young'un."

"Oh."

Missie could feel herself flush and hoped Willie didn't notice.

"It jest could be thet it'll arrive somewhere along the trail," Willie continued. "I talked to the wagon master and he says not to worry. Claims lots of young'uns are born on the way west. We have a midwife along, a Mrs. Kosensky. I hear tell she's delivered a number of babies. Still, iffen it were *my* wife . . ."

When he didn't finish his comment, Missie prompted, "If it were *your* wife . . . ?"

"Iffen it were my wife, I'd prefer thet she had a home to do the birthin' in—and a doc on hand, jest in case. In spite of Blake's bold words, I still got the feelin' thet he was jest a mite edgy 'bout it all, an' would much prefer to have thet young mother safely into a town and under some doc's responsibility when her time is come."

"He can't be too worried," Missie argued, "or he wouldn't have taken her on."

"From what I understand, the fact of the comin' baby wasn't told to Blake till all the arrangements were made—an' then he sure didn't want to turn them down. They'd already sold their farm back east."

"Then Mr. Blake can't really be faulted, him not knowing."

"Her man knew."

Missie turned away and busied herself with packing the coffeepot and frying pan. "I'm sure she'll be fine. I'll look her up today. What's her name, by the way?"

"Her man's name is Clay. I think it's John Clay, but I'm not right sure 'bout thet."

"Have you seen her?"

"Jest offhand like. Their wagon is one of the first in line. I saw them last night when I was takin' the horses down for water. He was helpin' her down from the wagon. I don't think she was out much yesterday."

"She'll get the feel of it," Missie said quickly, but she really wasn't as sure as she sounded. "Maybe she'll walk some today and I'll get a chance to meet her."

One of the trail guides was riding toward them on a rangy big roan with wild-looking eyes. Missie stared at the big-boned horse, thinking he looked as if he could handle anything, but she sure would not want to ride him.

The guide was calling out to each driver as he toured the circle, "Let's git those wagons hitched. Time to hit the trail."

The men moved almost as one toward the tethered horses. The women hurried with their tasks of repacking each item into the wagons, putting out the fires, and gathering their families together. Missie's preparations were already done, so she stood beside her wagon and observed the bustling scene before her.

Again she heard the crying baby. She loved babies and had lots of experience with them, growing up as she did in the Davis family. Still, she wasn't sure how wise or easy it would be to be heading west with one. She would offer the young mother a hand, maybe get some helpful hints on mothering for when her own baby arrived.

Her thoughts then turned to the other woman, the mother-to-be, hoping that today she would be able to meet her. She also hoped with all her heart that all would go well for the young woman. But Willie's expressed concern tangled itself about her like a confining garment. *I'll just have a chat with Mrs. Kosensky,* she thought. *She's had experience birthing babies, and she'll know what to do.*

Missie shook off her concerns and pushed away the nagging bit of guilt about not alerting Willie before they left. *I wasn't sure then,* she told herself again. *There was no point in putting another delay in front of poor Willie.* She climbed up on the wagon bench beside him and gave him a confident smile.

FOUR

Traveling Neighbors

That day Missie made a special effort to get acquainted with more of her traveling companions. Mrs. Collins was not hard to find. Missie simply followed the sound of the crying baby. She located the family a few wagons behind her own during the noon-hour break. Mrs. Collins was trying to prepare a midday meal for her hungry family with a small boy tugging at her skirt and the wailing infant being jostled on the young mother's hip.

Missie smiled and introduced herself. "We've already finished eating," she said, "and I was wondering if I could help with the baby while you prepare your meal."

"Oh, would ya?" Mrs. Collins said with great relief in her voice. "I'd sure appreciate it. Meggie's cryin' most drives me to distraction." She pushed the small boy from her. "Joey, please be patient. Mama will git yer dinner right away. Jest you sit down an' wait."

The boy plopped down on his bottom and also began to cry, his voice loud and demanding.

Missie reached for the baby, whose wails seemed to gain volume along with those of her brother, and walked back toward her own wagon. The poor mother would somehow have to cope with the howling Joey.

Missie walked back and forth beside their wagon, gently

bouncing the baby and singing softly to her. The crying subsided until only an occasional hiccough shook her tiny frame. Missie continued to rock and pace. When finally she checked little Meggie in her arms, she discovered the infant was sound asleep.

Missie returned to the mother, who was now busy clearing away the dishes and pots after having fed her husband and son. *I hope she took time to properly feed herself,* Missie thought.

Joey was sitting on a blanket, no longer crying, although the smudge of tears and trail dust still marked his cheeks. He looked very sleepy, and Missie wondered how long it would be until tears might overtake him again.

"Thank ya . . . I thank ya so much," Mrs. Collins said as she looked up from her tasks. "Ya can jest lay her down on the bed in the wagon."

Missie did so, having to move several items in order to find room for the tiny baby on the bed. She noticed that the Collins' living area was even smaller than the cramped quarters she and Willie shared—and there were four in their family.

Missie ducked out through the flap in the canvas. "Looks like Joey should get in a nap, too," she commented matter-of-factly.

"He's so tired," sighed the mother. Missie noted silently that she looked in need of a bed, also.

"I'll tuck him in," offered Missie, wondering if Joey would allow himself to be put to bed by a stranger.

To her surprise, he did not protest as she took his hand and helped him up. She started to lift him into the wagon but stopped long enough to dip a corner of her apron in water and wash the tear-streaked face. His face was warm and flushed, and Joey seemed to welcome the temporary coolness of the damp wash.

Missie laid Joey on the bed, trying to keep him far enough

away from Meggie that he wouldn't waken her. Even before Missie left the wagon, Joey's long eyelashes were fluttering in an attempt to fight off sleep. She was sure sleep would soon win and the boy would get the rest that would improve his disposition. She hoped that when he awakened, his young mother would have an easier time of it.

Missie left the wagon just as Mrs. Collins was stowing the last of her utensils. The wagons were about ready to move out for the afternoon's travel.

"Why don't you crawl in an' catch a bit of rest with the children?" Missie advised.

Mrs. Collins sighed deeply. "I think I will," she said, then turned to Missie. "I jest don't know how to thank ya." She blinked away tears. "Truth is, I was 'bout ready to give up."

"It'll get better," Missie promised, hoping sincerely that she was speaking the truth.

"Oh, I hope so . . . I truly hope so."

"We'll help."

"Thank ya." The young mother spoke with bowed head and trembling voice. "Yer very kind."

The call to "move out" came, and Missie stepped aside. "Best you get yourself settled," she encouraged. "I'll watch for you later."

Mrs. Collins nodded, trying valiantly to smile her gratitude. She climbed wearily into her wagon. Missie knew it was hot inside in the full heat of the day, but it was the most comfortable rest the overburdened mother would be able to find.

That afternoon Missie walked and rode in turn. When she was walking, she chatted with the other women and children who happened to be near. She met Mrs. Standard, a kind-looking woman with a sturdy frame and graying hair. She had a family of eight—five girls and three boys. It was the second marriage for Mr. Standard, Missie learned, and the woman was a bride of seven months—and a mother for only the same period of time. So the adjustment of suddenly caring for a brood of eight was indeed daunting. She had always wanted a family, but to acquire eight all at once—of various sizes, ages, and temperaments—was an awesome undertaking. Missie admired the woman for her enthusiasm and good humor as she faced all the changes in her life. Mrs. Standard had been a "town girl," so her marriage to the widower included facing the challenge of frontier life. He was convinced the rainbow's end must rest somewhere in the West, so Mrs. Standard had packed up his eight children and the few things of her own she could find room for and joined him on the long trek.

Mrs. Standard's usual walking companion was Mrs. Schmidt, a small, wiry woman who walked with a slight limp. She had three children—two nearly grown sons and a girl of eight.

Neither of the two women talked much as they walked. Missie assumed that just giving instructions to her large family was enough talking for Mrs. Standard, and Mrs. Schmidt didn't seem to have the need for much conversation. She was always busy *doing,* not talking. She gathered more firewood than she could ever manage to burn herself during the evening camping hours.

The women travelers included Mrs. Larkin, dark and unhappy looking, and Mrs. Page, who talked even faster than she walked—and she walked briskly. Whoever would care to listen—and some who didn't—had already been informed of every item Mrs. Page possessed, as well as the cost to purchase it, and how it had been obtained. Missie could endure only short sessions near the woman, then would drift farther away, thankful for the excuse of picking up firewood.

Mrs. Thorne, a tall, sandy-haired woman, walked stiff and upright, striding ahead in a rather manly way. Her three children walked just like their mother, their arms swinging freely at their sides, their steps long and brisk. Missie was sure Mrs. Thorne would have no difficulty taking on the West.

A young woman who had waved to Missie on her first day on the trail she now discovered to be Kathy Weiss, who was traveling west with her widowed father. She had a sunny smile and an easygoing disposition. She seemed a bit dreamy, and at times Missie wondered if she realized where this journey was taking her or if she just felt herself to be on an afternoon adventure in the woods that had simply gotten extended a bit.

Already Kathy had made friends with the young Mrs. Crane, a dainty porcelain-doll type of woman who appeared to be in a perpetual state of shock over what was happening to her. She was the train's fashion piece, refusing to dress herself in common yet practical cotton—the sensible thing to be wearing for this mode of travel and living. She wore instead stylish dresses and bonnets and impractical smart shoes. Her grooming every morning took far more time than her breakfast preparations. Missie smiled at such vanity, but her heart went out to the girl, who seemed so ill equipped for the journey and its unfamiliar end.

Missie sought out Mrs. Kosensky, the midwife, and she liked the stout motherly woman immediately. Her kind face and ready smile made Missie wish she could somehow ease the miles for the older woman, who had difficulties both with riding in the lurching wagon and walking alongside over the rutted trail.

Missie saw other small groups of women and children here and there, changing and interchanging with one another as the day wore on. She promised herself she would make an effort to get to know each one of them as quickly as possible, so she might take full advantage of friendships on the trail. Since they all had a common purpose and destination, it seemed to Missie that they should somehow be more similar, but she was amazed at the differences in personality, age, and variety of backgrounds that existed among them.

Missie watched carefully for the expectant mother Willie had mentioned. She was eager to meet the young Mrs. Clay, feeling a kinship with her, though her own secret would have to be guarded for a time. Missie sought the other woman each time she walked for a spell, but she still had not spotted her when the teams were again called to an early halt. As she had the day before, Missie almost stumbled into camp, so weary was she from the day's long trek. She deposited her few sticks of firewood beside the wagon and went to speak with Willie.

As Willie's hands moved to unharness the team, Missie caught sight of swelling blisters where the reins had irritated the skin on his fingers. She mentioned them, but Willie shrugged it off.

"They'll soon toughen up," he said without concern. "Only takes a few days. How're you?"

"Tired . . . and sore. But I think I'm faring better than some of them. I noticed poor Mrs. Crane was really limping when she climbed into her wagon back a piece."

"Is she the young peacock in the fancy feathers?"

Missie smiled. "Don't be too hard on her, Willie. She appreciates nice things."

"Well, she'd be a lot wiser to pack 'em away fer a while an' wear somethin' sensible."

"Maybe so, but she'll probably have to come to her own decision on that."

"Well, I'm jest glad you don't have sech notions," he said as he looked at her with a grin. "You'd best git some rest," Willie said, watching her closely as he prepared to move off with the horses. "Yer lookin' all done-in agin."

Missie did rest, though this time she determined not to fall asleep. With no trees of any size in the area this time, she settled herself against the wagon wheel and worked on some knitting. She noticed other women and children had found shade by the wagons and were finding some rest time, as well. In fact, the only one bustling about was Mrs. Schmidt, who was throwing more wood onto her already abundant pile.

The sounds of soft snoring drifted across from the direction of the next wagon. Missie looked over to see Mrs. Thorne stretched out full-length on the grass beside her wagon, one arm tucked beneath her head.

This in spite of some commotion around the Standard wagons. Mrs. Standard was busy tending the stubbed and bleeding toe of one of her stepchildren. He wailed as she washed the injured foot but soon quieted after he realized what a fine conversation piece that neat white bandage made. He hobbled off in search of someone who would appreciate his badge of courage.

Another Standard youngster rolled on the ground with the family dog. Mrs. Standard moved away from the yipping dog and laughing boy to lower herself to the ground with a heavy sigh. She removed her walking shoes and sat rubbing her feet. With her own feet suffering in empathy, Missie could imagine how they ached.

It seemed to her that the precious rest time moved as quickly as the sun dropped toward the horizon. Gradually things in the camp began to stir. Mrs. Schmidt was the first to have a fire going. But then she was going to need an early start if she was to burn up all that wood, Missie noted with a little smile as she stirred herself and laid aside her knitting. Smoke began to waft upward on the cooler evening air as supper plans began.

By the time Willie arrived, the fire was burning and the stew pot simmering. There was no need for Missie to make biscuits. Her mother's bread supply would last for a number of days yet, even though it would soon lose its freshness. Tonight, though, it was still soft and tasty. Missie savored each bite.

Henry ate with a hearty appetite, and Missie noticed that Willie wasn't far behind him in the amount of supper that he devoured.

"I've been thinking," said Missie, "we should have brought along one cow that was milking, instead of two that are months away from calving."

"Ya hankerin' fer some milk?" Willie wondered.

"Coffee and tea suit me fine, but just look at all of the youngsters around. They sure could do with some milk." Secretly, Missie realized that milk wouldn't be a bad idea for herself, as well, but she mentioned nothing about that fact.

Willie glanced around the campsite. "Yer right," he responded. "Seems to be young'uns aplenty. Seen any more of Mrs. Collins since noon?"

"No. She must ride in the wagon most of the time. Who could walk with two babies to carry? I was thinking maybe I'd slip over after we eat and see if she has some washing that has to be done."

Willie frowned slightly. "Don't mind ya bein' neighborly, Missie, but are ya sure ya aren't pushin' a bit hard? Ya still look a bit peaked an' weary to me."

"Speakin' of bein' neighborly," Henry suddenly chimed as he laid his empty plate aside, "think I'll do a little visitin' myself." He rose to his feet with sudden enthusiasm, obviously suppressing a grin as he sauntered off.

"Oh, I'm fine," Missie quickly assured Willie. "A couple more days on the trail, and I don't expect it'll bother me much at all."

Willie nodded a response of "I hope so," but the concern did not leave his eyes.

"I still didn't see Mrs. Clay," Missie said. "I watched for her all day."

"I think she stayed pretty close to the wagon. I saw John— that *is* his name—when I watered the horses. He says the sun has been a bit hard fer her to take."

"Do you suppose after we finish here we could walk over and see how they're doing?"

"Sure. Don't guess thet would be intrudin'." Willie reached for the Bible he had placed nearby and again turned to the passage in Isaiah that Clark had marked.

"'Fear thou not, for I am with thee,'" he read, then paused for a moment, staring at the page in front of him. "What does thet mean to you, Missie?"

Missie gazed off into the distance at the sun's warm glow still lingering in the west. She thought about the words, so familiar in one way but taking on new meaning as she and Willie were now on their own, heading away from home and family.

"I guess . . ." she said slowly, deliberately. "I guess it means that God is right here with us by our campfire. Oh, Willie!" she exclaimed. "We need Him so much. Not just for the physical journey . . . but for the inner self and strength and . . . I would be so lost without the Lord. It's hard enough leaving Pa and Mama and the family . . . but, Willie, if I'd had to leave God behind, too . . . I just couldn't go. I'm so glad He's coming with us. So glad."

Willie's arm went around Missie's shoulder and drew her close.

"Ya said what I'm feelin', too," he spoke quietly, his voice full of emotion. And when he was able to speak with control again, he led in a grateful prayer, including a petition for God's care and protection on Mrs. Clay and her coming baby.

FIVE

Rebecca Clay

Missie cleared away the meal while Willie carried water from the little stream to refill their water barrel. The couple then set out arm in arm to make the acquaintance of the Clays. It was a leisurely walk, and many times they paused to talk with fellow travelers. Missie introduced Willie to the women and children that she had met, and he in turn presented her to the men he already knew.

When they passed the Collins' wagon, Missie stopped to ask if she could help with any laundry. Mrs. Collins assured her they were quite all right for at least another day. Missie was secretly relieved and hoped it didn't show. She would gladly have helped the young woman if the need had been there, but her own body was still sore and weary from her two days on the trail. Maybe by the morrow she would begin to feel more like herself.

When eventually they came to the Clay wagon, Willie greeted John and proudly introduced Missie. John, in turn, called for Rebecca, who was inside the wagon. When she thought about it later, Missie wasn't sure what she had expected, but she was unprepared for her first glimpse of Rebecca as she pushed back the flap of the canvas and slowly stepped down, reaching for her husband's hand to assist her descent. Her face looked tired and so very young, but an easy smile brightened her countenance as she saw Missie. The long auburn-brown hair was swept back from a pale face and held fast with a dark green ribbon. Her eyes held glints of the same green. Rebecca was attractive, but her appeal was definitely more than that. Missie immediately found herself wanting to know her and become her friend.

As soon as Rebecca's feet were securely on the ground, she held out her hand to Missie.

"I'm Rebecca Clay." She spoke softly, controlled. "I'm so glad to meet you."

"And I'm Melissa LaHaye," Missie responded. She wasn't sure why she had said her given name, but somehow she felt Rebecca should know who she *really* was. "Folks all just call me Missie," she quickly added.

"And they call me Becky."

"That suits you," Missie said with a warm smile. She turned to Willie. "My husband, Willie—he's met your John."

"Yes, John told me. I've been anxious to meet you both, but I've been a bit of a baby for the past two days. I hope I'll soon be able to walk some with the rest of you. I'm sure your company would be much more enjoyable than my own." She extended her hand. "Please, won't you sit down. We have no chairs to offer, but those smooth rocks John rolled over aren't bad."

Missie joined in with Becky's chuckle as the four seated themselves on the rocks and settled in to talk. John replenished the fire. "Hope I can keep away some of those pesky mosquitoes," he said over his shoulder as he went for more kindling.

"An' jest where are you folks headin'?" Willie asked the first question on all lips of those traveling west. Missie found herself hoping the answer would bring good news of future neighbors.

"We travel with this train to Tettsford Junction, then rest

for a few days before joining a group going northwest," John answered. "My brother went out last year and sent word home that you never did see such good wheat land. He can hardly wait for us to get there so he can show it off. Says you don't even have to clear the land—just put the plow to it."

Missie found that hard to believe, but she had heard others tell the same story. She couldn't help but feel disappointment as she realized that the Clays would not be their neighbors after all.

"And you?" John Clay asked.

"We catch the supply train headin' south when we git to Tettsford. I've got me some ranch land in the southern hills."

"Ya like thet country?"

"It's pretty as a dream." Willie's eyes lit up as he got on his favorite subject for an audience who hadn't heard it all many times over. "All hills an' sky an' grassy draws. Not much fer trees in the area. The little valley where I'm plannin' to build has a few trees, but nothin' like we have where we come from."

"Understand there's no trees at all where we're heading," John noted.

"I can't imagine country without trees," Becky said slowly. Becky's voice sounded so wistful, Missie knew immediately that this deficiency would be a trial for the young woman.

Missie loved forests also and felt a sympathetic stirring inside, but she pushed it aside with a quick, "We'll get used to it."

Becky smiled. "I guess we will. Anyway, I suppose I'll be too busy to notice much."

The men had moved away to inspect John's harness. One section of the shoulder strap seemed to be rubbing a sore on his big black's right shoulder, John had explained, and he was anxious to find some way to correct the problem. As the men talked it over, Missie and Becky were left on their own.

"Did you leave a family behind?" Missie asked, thinking of her own parents.

"Only my father," answered Becky. "My mother died when I was fifteen."

"You don't look much more than fifteen now," Missie smiled.

Becky laughed. "Everyone thinks I'm still a youngster. Guess I just look like one. I wager I'm every day as old as you—I'll be nineteen next October."

Missie was surprised. "Why you *are* almost as old as me. When is your baby due?"

"In about two months. We're hoping all goes well so we'll be in Tettsford Junction by then. They have a doctor there, you know."

"They do?" said Missie. "I didn't know the town was that big."

"Oh, it's quite an important place, really. Almost all the wagon trains pass through it and then branch off in different directions."

"I sure find myself wishing that you were coming down our way," Missie said with sincerity.

Becky looked at her frankly. "I feel the same way. It wouldn't be half so scary if I knew I'd have you for a neighbor, even if you were nearly a day's ride away."

Both young women were silent for a few minutes. Missie toyed with the hem of her shawl while Becky poked without purpose at the fire.

"Missie," Becky spoke softly, "are you ever scared?"

Missie did not raise her eyes.

"About moving west?"

"Yes."

"I didn't *think* I was." Missie hesitated. "Willie was so excited, and I honestly thought I wanted to go, too. And I do, really I do. But I didn't know . . . that I'd . . . well, that I'd have such a hard time of it, that it'd hurt so much to leave Mama and Pa. I didn't think that I'd feel so . . . so empty." She stumbled over the words and finally raised her head and said deliberately, "Well, yes. Now I'm beginning to feel scared."

"Thanks for telling me, Missie. I'm glad I'm not the only one, because I feel like such a child about it all. I've never told anyone, not even John. I want so much for him to have his dream, but . . . sometimes . . . sometimes I fear I won't be able to make it come true for him, that my homesickness will keep him from being really happy."

Missie felt her eyes widen in surprise. "You feel homesick?"

"Oh yes."

"Even without leaving a mother behind?"

"Maybe even more so. My pa loved my mama so much it was awfully hard on him when he lost her. I was all he had, and when John came along, I . . . well, I fell so in love I couldn't think of anyone else." She stopped to take a deep breath. "So now I've . . . I've left Pa all alone," she finished in a rush.

Becky's eyes filled with tears. She brushed them away and continued, "If only he still had Mama, I wouldn't have this worry about him. I miss him . . . so very much. He's such a good man, Missie, so strong—big, muscular, tough. But inside, deep inside, Pa is so tender, so . . ." She took another breath. "Do you understand what I'm trying to say?"

Now it was Missie's eyes that filled with tears. She nodded. "Yes, indeed I do. I know just such a man, and I wouldn't be one bit surprised that he's crying silent tears for me just as often as I'm weeping for him. At least he has Mama and the other youngsters who are still at home."

"So you are lonesome, too?"

A quiet nod was Missie's answer.

"I expect it gets better."

"I hope so. I truly hope so," Missie said fervently. "I'm counting on God to make it so."

"You know . . . you talk to God?"

"Oh yes, without Him—"

"I'm so glad!" Becky exclaimed. "It's He who gives me daily courage, too. I'm not very brave . . . even *with* Him. But *without* Him, I'd be a downright coward."

Missie sniffed away her tears, and the two shared a laugh at Becky's confession.

"I'm glad I've got Willie," Missie said. "He has enough courage for both of us."

"So does John. He can see nothing but good in our future. Oh, I do hope that I won't let him down."

Missie reached over and squeezed the girl's hand. "You won't," she encouraged firmly. "You've got more than you allow yourself, or you wouldn't be here."

"Oh, Missie, I hope so."

"Are you afraid . . . about the baby?"

"A little. But I try not to think about things like that. Mostly I'm tired and a little sick from the sun and the motion of the wagon. I'll be so glad when I'm feeling well enough to walk."

"You must be careful not to walk too long at first."

"John thinks that walking will do me a lot of good. He says fresh air and good exercise is what I need. His ma had nine babies and never missed a day's work with any of them."

Well, good for John's ma, Missie wanted to say, but she held her tongue. Instead she said, "There's a midwife here. She's delivered lots of babies. She'll tell you if you should be pushing yourself and walking some."

"John told me about her, but I haven't met her yet."

"You'll like her, I'm sure. I met her today. She's just the kind of woman one would like to help with a birthing. I'll bring her around to meet you, if you'd like."

"Would you, Missie? I haven't felt up to seeking her out, and I do have a lot of questions. If my mama . . ." Becky did not finish but blinked quickly.

"I'll bring her by tomorrow, if I can," Missie assured her gently. Then she said, "When we left—Willie an' me—my pa gave us a special verse. We have sort of claimed it as ours, but no one really has any *special* claim on God. His promises are for all of His children. I'd like to share our verse with you. I hope it will be as special to you as it is to Willie and me. It comes from Isaiah." She paused, then quoted from memory, "'Fear thou not; for I am with thee: be not dismayed; for I am thy God: I will strengthen thee; yea, I will help thee; yea, I will uphold thee with the right hand of my righteousness.' That's an awful lot of promise for one verse to offer, but I feel sure that God really means it. He can—and will—be with us, in life or in death. I know He is with us through *everything*."

"Thank you, Missie, I really needed that truth. When you drop by on the morrow, would you do something for me? It's too dark to see right now, but I'd like you to show me where that verse is so I can read it for myself. Would you do that?"

"I'd be glad to."

The menfolk had gone on down to check the horses and rub some of Willie's ointment on the black's sore shoulder. The silence that followed Missie's words was broken only by the crackling of the fire. Missie found herself wishing she could tell Becky her own good news, but she held it back. Willie must be the first one to know. She must tell Willie—soon. It wasn't right to keep it from him. If only he wouldn't be worried. If she could just conquer her tiredness and perk up a bit. How thankful she was that she hadn't been troubled with bouts of morning sickness.

Becky interrupted her thoughts. "I'm afraid I have to confess to a lie, Missie. I'm not just a little afraid—I *am* scared—about the baby, about maybe not having a doctor, about the way I've been feeling. I don't know one thing about babies, Missie—not about their birthing or their care. The thought of maybe having that baby on this trip west nigh scares me to death, but John says . . ." She shook her head slowly and let the words hang.

Missie spoke quickly. "An' John's right. That baby will probably be born in Tettsford in a pretty bedroom with a doc there to fuss over him. But if . . . if the little one does decide to hurry it up a bit, then we have Mrs. Kosensky—about as good a woman as you'd find anywhere. Just you wait till you get to know her. She'll put your mind at ease. I'll fetch her around, first chance I get."

Becky summoned a smile. "Thanks, Missie. You must think me a real crybaby, carrying on so over an ordinary circumstance like a baby's coming. I'd like to meet Mrs. Ko . . . Ko . . . what's her name? Maybe she can even get me feeling better so I can do some walking with you. I feel like every bone in my body is turned to mush by the jarring, bouncing wagon." She smiled and rose. "The men should be coming back soon. Do you think they'd like some coffee?"

———

On Saturday night after supper, Trailmaster Blake called for a gathering of the wagon-train members.

"Life on a trek west can be a tad dull," he stated matter-of-factly, "so iffen any of ya can play anything thet makes a squeak, we'd 'preciate it iffen you'd bring it out."

Henry produced a guitar and Mr. Weiss a rather worn-looking fiddle. A time of singing around the fire was arranged, and folks joined in heartily, humming the tunes when they did not know the words. Some of the children jumped or skipped or swayed to the music in their own version of a folk dance.

What Mr. Weiss could accomplish on his well-used fiddle was quite remarkable, and Henry was rather adept at keeping up with him. Henry was also blessed with a pleasant singing voice, and he led the group in one song after another, some of them camp choruses and others favorite hymns. Missie loved every minute of it, and the singing brought back memories of their little congregation back home worshiping together. She decided Henry's healthy appetite was well worth feeding, and she determined to always be ready with generous second helpings.

Far too soon for Missie, Mr. Blake stood and waved his hand for attention.

"Thank ya, men . . . thank ya. You've done a fine job. Now it's gittin' late and time to be turnin' in. 'Sides, the mosquitoes are 'bout as hungry as I've ever seen 'em." He waved a few away from his face.

"Tomorrow, bein' Sunday, the train will stay to camp. Me, I'm not a religious man, but a day of rest jest plain makes sense—both fer the animals an' fer us people. Now, iffen you who are religious are hankerin' fer some kind of church service, I'm leavin' ya on yer own to do the plannin'. I'm no good at sech things. Fact is, I plan on spendin' tomorrow down at yonder crik, seein' iffen I can catch me some fish." He looked around the group. "Now, then, are there any of you who'd be wantin' church?"

Quite a few hands were raised.

"Fine . . . fine," Mr. Blake said. "Klein, ya figurin' thet you can take charge?"

Henry looked a little nonplussed but nodded his assent, and the meeting was dismissed.

Henry then spent some time calling upon his wagon neighbors in preparation for the morning service. A few did not wish to take part, but most were eager to worship together on the Lord's Day.

Willie was appointed to read the Scripture, and Henry himself took charge of the singing. Mr. Weiss could play hymns on his old violin with even more feeling than he played the lively dance tunes and folk songs, and everything was set.

———————

Sunday dawned clear and warm. The service had been set for nine so it would be over before the sun was too high and hot in the sky. The people gathered in a grove of trees near the stream and settled themselves beneath the protective branches on logs that Willie and Henry had cut and placed there for that purpose.

They began with a hearty hymn-sing, Henry leading out in his clear baritone voice. Kathy Weiss taught the group a new song—simple and short but with a catchy tune. Many hands clapped in accompaniment when they were not occupied with slapping mosquitoes.

After the final triumphant stanza of "Amazing Grace," Henry indicated the singing had concluded and asked Mr. Weiss to lead the group in prayer. He did so with such fervor that Missie was reminded of home.

Anyone who wished was invited to tell of finding God's presence on the trail. One by one, several stood to express their thanks to God for His leading, for strength, for assurance in spite of fears, for incidents of protection along the way. Missie and Becky exchanged glances and meaningful smiles.

After the last voluntary testimony had been shared, Willie read the Scripture. He had chosen the passage about Jesus feeding the multitudes with only a small boy's lunch. Missie was sure that others caught the special significance of trusting God to provide for them and to protect them in their travels together. The group listened carefully as Willie's voice presented the words from the Bible and his confidence in the promises of God. When he closed the Book there were many nods and "amens."

Though their wilderness setting gave no hint of a church building, the time of worship had been just as meaningful as if they'd had a roof over their heads and a church bell tolling. As the group scattered to their own campsites, they shook Henry's hand and thanked him for a job well done. Some suggested another hymn-sing around the fire that night, and so it was arranged.

The Sunday service and Sunday night hymn-sing became even more popular with the wagon-train members than the Saturday night gathering. As the weeks went by, some of those who had not been interested in joining the Sunday crowd for their worship time found themselves washing their faces, putting on clean clothes, brushing the trail dust off their boots, and heading for whatever spot had been set aside for that week's service. Missie and Willie were thrilled to see the interest grow. The folks appeared to yearn for that restful time of worship and sharing on Sunday.

Mr. Blake, on the other hand, was left to his own choice of Sunday activity, whether it was hunting, fishing, or just lying in the shade. Missie noticed him on one particular Sunday morning, though, when he had chosen to simply hang around camp. It looked suspiciously as if he were listening.

Tedious Journey

Day after long day rolled and bounced by in mostly tiresome predictability. Even the weather seemed monotonous. The sun blazed down upon them with only an occasional shower to bring temporary relief.

But gradually the travelers adjusted to the journey. Bodies still ached at the end of the day, but not with the same intense painfulness. Blisters now had been replaced by calluses. Occasionally a horse would become lame, and their drivers watched with great care and concern for any serious signs of injury to their animals.

One family, the Wilburs, had been forced to pull aside and retire from the train due to an injured horse that simply could not continue. Mr. Blake thoughtfully detoured the train about two miles out of its way in order to drop the young couple off at a small army outpost. The sergeant in charge promised he'd send a few of his men back with Mr. Wilbur to retrieve his stranded wagon and lead the horses to the safety of the fort. At the earliest future date, the Wilburs would be escorted to the nearest town. Missie could have wept when she saw their expressions of intense disappointment as the train moved on without them.

Some minor mishaps during the journey reminded them all of the need for care and caution. One of the Page children had been burned when playing too near a cooking fire. Mr. Weiss, the train's blacksmith, had been kicked by a horse he was attempting to shoe, but fortunately nothing was broken. Mrs. Crane's ankle had twisted badly as she attempted to scale a steep hill in her fashionable shoes, and she was confined to the family wagon far longer than she would have liked. A few of the young children were plagued with infected mosquito bites, and occasional colds made one or the other miserable for a time. But, all in all, everyone was adjusting quite well to life on the trail.

As the group slowly made its way westward, the country-side began changing. Missie tried to determine what made it seem so different—so foreign to her from the farming community she had left. The trees were smaller and unlike most of the trees she had been used to. The hills appeared different, too. Perhaps it was the abundance of short undergrowth that clung to their slopes. Whatever the differences, Missie also realized she was getting farther and farther away from her home and those she loved. The now-familiar feeling of lonesomeness still gnawed and twisted within her. Once in a while she was forced to bite her lip to keep the tears from overflowing onto her cheeks. She must try harder, pray more. And as she walked or worked she repeated over and over to herself the blessed promise of Isaiah. Her greatest ally was busyness, and she tried hard to keep her hands and her mind occupied.

Missie visited Becky often, and she had kept her promise to introduce her to the midwife, Mrs. Kosensky. The capable woman had dismissed husband John's advice that Becky walk more and cautioned her to be careful about the amount of activity she involved herself in each day. Now that she was feeling better, Becky wasn't sure she liked the restrictions but obeyed the new instructions, nonetheless.

Missie found plenty of opportunity to help Mrs. Collins

with the care of her two young children. She often took the baby girl to visit Becky so she might have some experience in the care and handling of a baby.

Try as she might to keep her thoughts on the future and the adventure ahead, Missie found herself continually recalling the events of the day as they would be taking place "back home." *Today Mama will be hanging out the wash, all white and shimmering in the sun,* or *today Pa will be making his weekly trip into town.* Or on Sunday, *the whole family is in the buggy and heading for the little log church. They're going to meet and worship with the neighbors—people I've known all my life—and Parson Joe.* She could almost hear his voice as he would preach the sermon and the "amens" accompanying his presentation of truth from Scripture. And she could close her eyes and see her dear sister Clae's smile as she gazed with love and pride at her husband behind the simple pulpit.

And so Missie went through each day. Her weary but gradually strengthening body traveled with the other pilgrims of the wagon train, but her spirit soared "back home," where she shared the days' activities with those she had left behind.

She realized with surprise as she prepared their evening meal that they had been on the trail for almost four weeks. In some ways it had seemed forever; in others, it seemed not so long at all. But after this amount of time, why was she still feeling that inner homesickness and loneliness? Time, she had thought, would lessen the pain, ease the burden of loneliness. How long would it require for her to be at peace with her circumstances?

As Missie's body ached less by each day's end, it seemed that her spirit ached more. How she missed them—her family and friends. How good it would be to feel her mama's warm embrace or her pa's hand upon her shoulder. How she would welcome the teasing of Clare and Arnie, enjoy watching the growing up of her younger sister, Ellie. And Luke in his soft lovableness—how she ached to hug his little body. Would she even recognize him when she saw him again—whenever that time might come? *Oh, dear God,* she prayed over and over, *please make me able to bear it.*

With all her might, Missie fought to hide her suffering from Willie. But in so doing, she didn't realize how much of her true self she was withholding from him. She often felt Willie's eyes upon her, studying her face. He fretted over her weariness and continually checked to be sure she was feeling all right, was not overworking, was eating properly.

The truth was, Missie was not feeling well. Apart from her deep homesickness, she also was suffering with nausea and general tiredness. But she hid it from Willie. *It's not the right time yet. Willie would just worry,* she kept telling herself. But she sensed—and did not like—the strain that was present between them.

Each day followed the last one in very similar fashion. The LaHayes always rose early. Missie prepared breakfast for Willie and Henry while they checked and watered the animals and prepared them for the new day's travel. They ate, packed up, and moved out. At noon they took a short break, and Missie again prepared a quick meal.

When they stopped at the end of the day, there was the fire to start, the supper to be cooked, and the cleaning up to be done. Very little fresh food now remained, so Missie had to resort to dried and home-canned foods. She was fast wearying of the limited menu. She wondered if it was as distasteful to Willie and Henry as it was to her. What wouldn't she give to be able to sit down to one of her mother's appetizing meals with garden produce and fresh-baked bread? She shook her head quickly and determined to put her mind on other things.

The amount of walking Missie included in each day's travel depended on the terrain and the intensity of the heat. Becky Clay did not attempt to walk very much at all. John refrained from prodding her to do more than she felt comfortable doing after Mrs. Kosensky had told him that all women were not as hardy as his mother. Becky did welcome her short episodes with the other women, though she had to be careful not to overdo.

The travelers began to know one another as individuals, not just faces. For some, this was good. Mrs. Standard and Mrs. Schmidt seemed to accept and enjoy each other more every day. They hoped to be close neighbors when the journey ended.

Kathy Weiss and Tillie Crane also became close friends. Kathy spent many hours with Anna, as well, the oldest of the five Standard girls. But Anna and Tillie shared no common interest and seemed to have no desire to spend time in each other's company. In turn, Mrs. Standard appeared to enjoy Kathy and embraced her right along with her own recently acquired brood of eight. Missie imagined that Mrs. Standard would have been willing to take almost anybody into the family circle.

Henry, too, was a welcome visitor around the Standard campfire. Missie often wondered if the attraction for him was one of the young girls or the motherly Mrs. Standard. Henry, whose mother had died when he was young, no doubt yearned for the care and nurturing he had missed growing up.

As well as fast friendships among the travelers, there were also a few frictions. Mrs. Thorne still carried herself stiff and straight, never making an effort to seek out anyone's company. Neither by word nor action did she invite anyone to share time or conversation with her. There were no neighborly visits over a coffee cup around the Thornes' fire.

Most of the travelers tried to avoid the chattering Mrs. Page, but she had a way of popping up out of nowhere and making it virtually impossible for one to escape without being downright rude. It seemed she would have cozied up to a cactus if she had thought it had ears. Yet even Mrs. Page was not willing to share her goodwill with everyone.

Missie never did know what had started it in the first place, but for some reason a deep animosity had grown between Mrs. Page and Mrs. Tuttle. Mrs. Tuttle was a widow, traveling west with her brother. Unlike Mrs. Page, she had very little to say, but what she did say was often acidic and painful. So she, too, was avoided but for the opposite reason from the voluble Mrs. Page.

The woman simply did not know when to stop her running commentary on this and that. Her elaborations on any subject included expounding on the reason Mrs. Tuttle was going west. According to Mrs. Page, a trapper was waiting at the other end of the trail, having made a proposal of sorts by mail. Mrs. Page announced she was sure the trapper was "trapped," that if he'd been able to get any kind of look at Mrs. Tuttle's stern face, he would have preferred solitude. So the war waged on.

Most of the battles between the two women were carried on through messengers. "You tell Jessie Tuttle thet iffen she doesn't learn how to crack the ice on thet face of hern, she'll lose thet trapper as soon as she finds 'im."

"You tell Mrs. Page"—Jessie Tuttle would not allow herself to use Mrs. Page's first name, Alice—"thet when she cracked the ice off'n her own face, she did a poor job of it. Now the button fer her mouth don't hold it shut none."

Of course, the emissaries never did deliver the messages, but it wasn't necessary for them to do so. The insults were always spoken loudly within earshot of the opposing party. The running battle provided no real alarm and even a small measure of amusement for the other members of the wagon train. There was little enough to smile at, so even a neighborly squabble was welcome.

Occasional meetings of all adult members of the train provided opportunity for the wagon master to give reports on progress, or to issue a new order, or to explain some new situation. Even such a meeting was looked upon as a pleasant diversion from the mundane and the usual.

Mr. Blake now told the travelers he was pleased with their progress and that they were right on schedule. His concern was the large river they were approaching. They would reach the ford in four days' time at the current rate of travel. He was sure the river would be down, making the crossing an easy one. High water from heavy rains was the only possible obstacle that could hamper the crossing, Mr. Blake said, and they had been particularly blessed with sunny, clear days. Once across the Big River, as it was called by the local Indians, they were well on their way to their final destination.

Everyone seemed to rejoice at Mr. Blake's news, but deep down, Missie knew she did not. Within her was a secret wish that the river would not be fordable and that Willie would decide to turn around and go back home.

Willie obviously did not share her yearnings to return. At the wagon master's encouraging announcement, he had cheered as loudly as any of the travelers. Missie did notice there were a few other women who had remained silent—Becky, Sissie Collins, and Tillie Crane among them.

Missie was quiet on their way back to the wagon, but at first Willie was too energized to notice.

"Jest think," he enthused, "only four more days an' we cross the Big River, an' then . . . then we'll *really* start to roll!"

Missie nodded and tried to work up a smile for Willie's sake.

"Are ya still worryin' 'bout Becky?" Willie queried, trying to look into her face and no doubt hoping for some reasonable explanation for Missie's restraint.

"Yeah, kind of," Missie responded, feeling the answer was both safe and, to a measure, truthful.

"But there's something else . . . isn't there? I've been feelin' it fer a long time. Aren't ya feelin' well, Missie?"

It was asked with such genuine concern that Missie knew somehow she must attempt to put Willie's mind at ease. This wasn't the way she would have planned to break the news to Willie. She had pictured the intimacy of their own fireside of an evening, or the closeness of their shared bed in the privacy of their covered wagon. But here they were walking over a rutted dusty path with people before, behind, and beside them. There seemed almost no way for her to speak low enough so she wouldn't be heard by others. Yet she knew she must tell him.

"I've been wanting to tell you, but the time never seemed right," she said quietly. She took a long breath. "Willie . . . we're going to have a baby, too."

Willie stopped walking and reached for Missie, his face very sober.

"Ya aren't joshin'?"

"No, Willie."

"An' yer sure?"

"Quite sure."

Willie stood silently for a moment, then shook his head. "I'm not sure thet wagon trains an' babies go together."

For a brief moment Missie hoped maybe this would give Willie a reason to head for home, but she quickly pushed the selfish thought from her and managed a smile. "Oh, Willie, don't fuss. We'll be in our own place long before our baby ever arrives."

"Ya sure?"

"Of course. How long you think we're going to be on this trail, anyway?"

The expression on Willie's face suddenly changed and he let out a shout. Missie reached out to hush him before he'd announced his news to the whole wagon train. Willie stopped whooping and hugged Missie tightly. Relief flooded over her. He was truly excited about it—there was no doubting it.

Suddenly Missie wanted to cry. She wasn't sure why, but she felt such a joy at telling her news to Willie, seeing his exuberance, and feeling his strong arms about her. She had been wrong to withhold it from him. A great wave of love for Willie washed over her. She would go to the ends of the earth with him if he wanted her to.

They laughed and cried together as Willie held her in his arms and kissed her forehead and her hair. Their fellow travelers had passed on by and left them alone for the moment.

"So this is why ya haven't been yerself," Willie murmured into her hair. "We gotta take better care of ya. Ya need more rest an' a better diet. I'll have to git fresh meat oftener. Ya shouldn't be doin' so much. Ya'll overdo. I was so scared, Missie, thet maybe you'd changed yer mind, thet ya didn't want to go out west . . . or thet maybe ya didn't even love me anymore . . . or thet ya had some bad sickness . . . or . . . oh, I was scared. I jest prayed an' prayed an' here . . . here . . ." She could hear the emotion in his voice.

Missie had not realized before what her long days of listlessness and homesickness had meant for Willie. She must not hold back from him again.

"I'm sorry, Willie," she whispered, "I didn't know that you were feeling . . . were thinking all those things. I'm sorry."

"Not yer fault. Not yer fault at all. I'm jest so relieved, thet's all. Still sorry thet yer not feelin' well—but we'll take care of ya. After all, it's fer a *very* good reason!"

"I'm glad that you're happy—"

But Missie didn't get a chance to finish her sentence. Willie stopped her as he drew her close. "Everything is gonna be fine now, Missie. Ya should be feelin' better soon. We'll have a chat with Mrs. Kosensky. We'll make sure thet ya git lots of rest. An' 'fore ya know it, you'll be fine, jest fine."

"Willie? Willie, there's something else, too. True, I've been feeling a mite down. But I think the true reason for me . . . my . . . ah . . . well, the way I feel is just lonesomeness, Willie. Just lonesomeness for Mama and Pa and . . ." Missie could not continue. The tears ran freely.

Willie held her close against him. He stroked her hair and gently wiped the tears from her cheek.

"Why didn't ya tell me, Missie?" he said at last. "I woulda understood. I've been missing those left behind, too. Maybe I couldn't have eased yer sorrow none, Missie, but I'da shared it with ya." He tipped her face and gently kissed her. "I love ya, Missie."

Why had she been so foolish? Why had she hugged her hurt to herself, thinking that Willie would not understand or care? She should have told him long ago and accepted the comfort of his arms. Missie clung to him now and cried until her tears were all spent. Surely there was some healing in shared heartache, in cleansing tears. At length she was able to look up at Willie and smile again.

Willie kissed her on the nose and gave her another squeeze.

"Hey," he said suddenly, "we gotta git this little mama off to bed. No more late nights fer you, missus. An' not quite so much walkin' an' doin', either."

"Oh, Willie," protested Missie, "the walking is a heap easier for me than that bumpy old wagon."

"Ya reckon so?"

"I reckon so. It's not exactly a high-springed buggy, you know."

Willie chuckled as he led Missie carefully across the clearing to their wagon.

"Mind yer step, now," he said earnestly as he boosted her up. "Mustn't overdo it."

"Oh, Willie," Missie laughed in exasperation. But she knew she was in for a lot of babying in the future. Well, maybe it wouldn't be so bad if he just wouldn't overdo it. She smiled to herself and ducked to enter their canvas doorway.

SEVEN

Rain

The next morning Missie could tell Willie was still in a state of bliss as he climbed out of the wagon to begin a new day.

She had watched him pull the gray wool shirt over his head with all those buttons from waist to neck, then tuck it quickly into the coarse denim pants that made up his trail clothing. He had glanced over at her and, seeing she was awake, gave her a delighted grin, then quickly sobered as he told her to stay in bed for a bit longer. She'd need extra rest. She smiled sleepily, then suggested that if the day got too hot, he'd probably want to change the shirt for a cotton one. He nodded, raised his suspenders, and snapped them into place. At the entrance to the wagon he stopped to pull on his calf-high leather boots. He shrugged his way out of the canvas doorway and headed out to get the team ready for the day's journey. He went with an even jauntier step and cheerier whistle than usual. Missie knew he was pleased about the coming baby. She also knew he was thinking, *Four more days to the Big River!*

To Missie, it meant four more days to the point of no return. She tried to shake off her melancholy for Willie's sake and went about her morning chores with a determined cheerfulness. Today, if she had the opportunity, she *might* reveal the good news of her coming baby to Becky. They could plan together.

Willie stopped the team often that morning to give Missie opportunities for walking—and then to check that she hadn't already walked far enough. She humored him by walking for a while and then welcoming a ride when he suggested it. She actually could have traveled by foot most of the morning. The walking had bothered her less each day, but there was no use worrying Willie.

In the afternoon a chill came with the wind, and dark storm clouds gathered on the horizon. The whole wagon train seemed to be holding its breath in unison. It was soon apparent to all that this storm would not pass over with just a shower. Still, the team drivers and their apprehensive womenfolk entertained the hope that the rain would not last for long. The animals seemed to sense the approaching storm, too, and by the time the thunder and lightning commenced, they were already nervous and skittish.

The rain came lightly at first. The women and children scrambled for the cover of the wagons, while the men wrapped themselves in canvas slickers and drove on through the storm.

But rather than decreasing in intensity, the storm with its dark clouds swirling above seemed angry and vindictive as the waters poured down. Soon the teams were straining to pull the heavy high-wheeled wagons through the deepening mud. Those fortunate enough to have extra horses or oxen hitched them to their wagons, also.

The guides ranged back and forth, watching for trouble along the trail. It came all too soon. One of the lead wagons slid while going down a slippery steep slope, bouncing a wheel against a large rock. The wooden spokes snapped with a sickening crack. The wagon lurched and heaved, though fortunately it did not tip over. Mr. Calley somehow kept the startled horses from bolting.

The teams following had to maneuver around the crippled

wagon, slipping and sliding their way down the rocky hill and onto even ground. As soon as the last wagon was safely down the badly rutted hillside, Mr. Blake ordered a halt. They should have had many more miles of traveling for the day behind them, but it was useless to try to go on. The Big River would have to wait.

The sodden wagons gathered into their familiar circular formation, and the teams, with steam rising from their heaving sides, were unhitched. Some of the men went back up the hill to help the unfortunate Calley family. Their wagon could not be moved until the broken wheel was mended. The men labored in the pouring rain, attempting to raise the corner of the wagon by piling rocks and pieces of timber underneath. The Calleys would have to spend the night at a little distance from the rest of the camp.

While Willie and Henry were gone, Missie wrapped a heavy shawl about her and went in search of firewood. The other women and children were seeking material for their fires, as well, and the rain meant there was very little to be found. Missie felt wet and muddy and cross as she scrambled for bits and pieces of anything she thought might burn. At one point she heard a commotion and then a voice shouting, "You tell Jessie Tuttle thet once a body is headin' fer a stick of firewood, thet body is entitled to it." Missie smiled in spite of herself. The two were at it again!

Only the forward-thinking Mrs. Schmidt did not have to join the others in the dispiriting search. Her ever-abundant supply of dry wood was unloaded from under the wagon seat. Missie wondered why she hadn't had the presence of mind to plan ahead, as well.

Missie finally had gathered what she hoped would be enough to cook a hot meal, then slogged her way back through the mud to her wagon. The fire was reluctant, at best, but

Missie finally coaxed a flame to life. It sputtered and spit and threatened to go out, but Missie encouraged it on. The coffee never did boil, but the reheated stew was at least warm, and the near-hot coffee was welcome to shivering bodies.

Missie cleaned up in a halfhearted manner, and they crawled into their canvas home on wheels to get out of their wet clothing and into something warm and dry. It was far too early to go to bed, even though the day had been a strenuous one. Willie lit a lamp and settled down beside it to bring his journal up-to-date. Missie picked up her knitting, but her fingers were still too cold to work effectively. At length she gave up and pulled a blanket around herself for warmth. Willie lifted his head to look at her and started fretting again.

"Ya chilled? Ya'd best git right into thet bed—don't want ya pickin' up a cold. Here, let me help ya. I'll go see what I can find for a warm stone fer yer feet." He tucked the blanket more closely around Missie, right to the chin, and started to reach for his coat.

"Don't go back out in the rain—please, Willie," Missie begged. "My feet aren't that cold. They'll be warm in no time. I'll just slip on a pair of your woolen socks." And Missie did so immediately so Willie could see she meant what she had said.

It was too early to go to sleep, Missie knew. She also knew it was unwise to protest being tucked in, so she snuggled under the blanket, and gradually the chill began to leave her bones. She even began to feel drowsy.

Willie finished his journal entries and picked up a leather-covered edition of *Pilgrim's Progress* that had been a wedding gift from Missie's schoolchildren. Missie murmured, "If you don't mind, would you read it aloud?"

Willie read, his voice and the familiar story lulling her toward a sense of well-being, and the long evening somehow passed.

The rain continued to fall, splattering against the canvas of the wagon. Before lying down to sleep beside Missie, Willie checked carefully all around the inside of their small enclosure to make sure there were no leaks. Then in a very few minutes Missie knew by his breathing that he slept. She wished she could fall asleep as easily, but instead she lay and listened to the rain. Again her thoughts turned to home.

She used to love to listen to the rain pattering on the window as she snuggled down beneath the warm quilt her mama had made. The rain had always seemed friendly then, but somehow tonight it did not seem to be a friend at all. She shivered and moved closer to Willie. She was thankful for his nearness and his warmth. And his confidence.

When Missie awakened the next morning, the rain was still falling. Puddles of water lay everywhere, and the shrubbery and wagons dripped steady little streams in the damp morning air. Willie arrived just as Missie was about to crawl down from the wagon, wondering what in the world she would ever do about a fire. Instructing her to stay where she was, he managed to get a fire going and make some coffee and pancakes. He served Missie in the covered wagon, ignoring her protests.

"No use us both gittin' wet and cold," he reasoned. " 'Sides, Mr. Blake hasn't decided yet whether we move on or jest sit tight."

But they all knew of Mr. Blake's concern about reaching the Big River before the waters were swollen with the rain. So in spite of the mud, he ordered them to pack up and move out as usual.

Willie was already soaking wet as he climbed up onto the wagon seat and urged the balking horses out. He told Missie to make as comfortable a place for herself as she could and to stay under the canvas.

It was tough going. The wagons slipped and twisted through the mire. Wheels clogged up and had to be freed from their burdens of mud. Teams and drivers were worn out in only a few hours' time. When one poor horse finally fell and needed a great deal of assistance to regain his footing, Mr. Blake called a halt. It was useless to try to travel farther under such conditions.

Missie didn't know whether to feel relief or dismay when their wagon creaked to a stop. The rain had slackened a bit, so she wrapped her shawl closely about her and went on the inevitable search for firewood. But when Willie returned some time later, Missie still had not succeeded in getting a fire going. She was close to tears and felt like a complete failure. The wood just would not burn. Willie took charge, talking Missie into changing out of her wet clothes. He dared to beg some hot water from Mrs. Schmidt, whose fire was burning cheerily—as if it were sticking its tongue out at the whole camp. Mrs. Schmidt seemed pleased—though possibly a bit smug—to share her hot water. Missie made tea in the confines of the wagon, and she, Willie, and Henry enjoyed the hot refreshment, along with their biscuits from yesterday.

Still the rain continued. Missie went back to her knitting while Willie mended a piece of harness. When that was done, he pulled out his journal, but this source of activity was soon exhausted, as well. He picked up the John Bunyan volume again and attempted to read, but eventually restlessness drove him from the wagon and out into the rain, muttering an excuse about checking on the teams and the cows.

With Willie gone, the afternoon dragged even more for Missie. She was on the verge of venturing forth herself when she heard Willie return. At his call from the back of the wagon,

Missie raised the tent flap. He handed her a bundle, the Collins' baby.

"Their wagon is leakin'," he explained. "There ain't a dry place to lay the young'uns. I'll be right back with the boy."

Missie busied herself with unwrapping the baby. True to his word, Willie was soon there at the canvas opening with little Joey in tow. When baby Meggie fussed, Missie cheerfully spent the time hushing her, rocking her back and forth and coaxing her to settle into a comfortable position. Willie entertained Joey, helping him make a tiny cabin with small sticks. Then he read to him out of *Pilgrim's Progress,* and even though the young boy could not possibly understand much of the story, he listened intently. Missie finally managed to get the baby to sleep. She joined Willie and Joey, now involved in a little-boy game with sticks and stones.

Sissie Collins came by later to check on her children and nurse the baby. Willie made the rounds of the camp to see if there was anyone else needing a helping hand.

When the long day came to an end, they drank the remains of the now-cold tea and ate some cold meat with the remaining biscuits.

Willie moved into the other wagon with Henry so Sissie and her two little ones could stay with Missie in drier surroundings.

As Missie went to sleep again with the sound of the rain on the canvas, she wondered if it would ever stop. How could they possibly endure another day such as this?

But they did. At times the rain slackened to a mere drizzle, and at other times it poured. Each time the rain slowed, Missie pulled on her shawl and left the confines of the wagon. But actually there was little place to walk around and stretch her cramped legs. The ground around the site looked like a lake with only a few high spots still showing through. At first Missie tried to stay to the high ground, then giving up with a shrug, she sloshed about through the water.

Finally even Mrs. Schmidt ran out of firewood, so the men made a concerted effort to find something farther out that would burn. Eventually it was decreed that one fire, built under a stretched-out canvas, would be shared by the whole camp. The women took turns, three or four at a time, hastily preparing something hot for their families.

The Collins family wasn't the only one having problems with leaking canvas. Other wagons, too, were wet—inside and out. Families were doubling up and sharing quarters wherever possible.

The rain heightened the tension between the two female antagonists. But the howls of outrage from Mrs. Page and the biting retorts of Mrs. Tuttle were often the very thing that kept the rest of the company sane. It was a nice diversion to be able to chuckle—even at one another.

On the fifth day the sky began to clear, and the sun broke through on the dripping and miserable wagon train.

The travelers, too, came out, quickly stringing lines and hanging clothing and blankets to dry. The ground remained wet, and it could be days before the stands of water disappeared and even a longer time before the ground would be dry enough to allow the wagons to roll ahead once again.

Missie felt somewhat like Noah as she descended from her wagon. There was water everywhere. How good it would be to see the dry land appear and the horses kick up dust. Oh, to be on the move again!

Mr. Blake clearly felt impatient, too, but his many years of experience on the trail no doubt told him it would be useless to try to travel on in the mud. No, they'd have to wait, he told them, explaining that with the rains of the past few days, the Big River would be impossible to cross very soon anyway.

They'd been delayed, but they'd just take the problems one day at a time. "We'll be there a'fore ya know it." He finished his announcement with a tip of his hat to the glum faces before him.

Missie wondered how much time "a'fore ya know it" actually meant. But her first duty was to collect firewood, wet though it might be, and lay it out to dry for future use. She would not be caught short again if she could at all help it.

EIGHT

The Big River

For six days Mr. Blake kept the wagons in their camp circle. He no doubt would have held them longer, foreseeing the unwelcome surprise that probably awaited them at the Big River, but the growing impatience to be rolling again made the group restless. The ground in the immediate vicinity was dry enough to travel, and the risk of tempers flaring from tense nerves and idle hands overcame his reluctance to face a swollen river. On day seven he called for the travelers to break camp.

But those six days had not been lost in inactivity. Harnesses had been repaired, wagons reinforced, canvases carefully patched and oiled where the relentless rain had found a way inside. Clothes had been washed and mended, blankets aired, and bodies scrubbed. A hunting party returned to camp with two deer, and the venison fed the whole camp. The fresh meat was a welcome change from their dried and canned diet.

The scent of frying steak wafted over the camp that last evening, bringing a light spirit and unusually intent interest in supper preparations. Some women had found a berry patch and in short order stripped it clean. The tangy fruit made that special meal seem like a banquet. All were refreshed and looking forward to beginning the journey again.

It took the train three days to reach the Big River. When they finally arrived, Mr. Blake found exactly what he had been afraid they would face—a current far too strong and swift to allow safe wagon passage. He again called a meeting and explained the situation to the entire group. Another camp would have to be made beside the river until the waters subsided. The determined but weary travelers were all disappointed, but even the most impatient agreed with the decision.

So camp was set up, and the families again tried to establish some sort of daily routine to keep boredom from overtaking them. The men formed regular hunting parties, and the women and older children again ranged out in search of berries. Missie spent a part of each day gathering wood, as did the other women who did not have children to assign to the task. As she gleaned her daily supply, she also added to her stack of surplus piled under her wagon. If the rains should come again, Mrs. Schmidt would not be the only one who was prepared, she told herself firmly.

Some of the older ladies began to suspect Missie was "in the family way." Although no comments were made, Missie often noticed the motherly glances of interest and concern that came her way. The birth of her baby was almost five months away by Missie's reckoning, and that seemed like a long, long time into the future. Far longer than anyone should worry about, she silently told herself.

Missie found herself searching out the company of Becky Clay. There was no doubt in anyone's mind as to Rebecca's condition, and the other women found many little ways to make the young woman's work load lighter. Dry sticks were tossed onto her pile as the women walked by with their load of wood, extra food was presented at her campfire, and her pail went along to the stream for water with someone who had a free hand.

For Becky's sake, Missie felt extra concern over the travel delay. She was hoping along with Becky that they would reach

Tettsford Junction and the doctor in time. Each day Missie prayed and hoped that by some miracle the swollen waters would be down and the train could be on its way. But just when the river appeared to be receding, somewhere along its banks another storm would raise the waters again. Rafting the wagons to the other side was out of the question in this deep, swift river, and day after day passed with the wagons still unable to cross.

On the fifteenth day by the Big River, the whole camp came to life as news of another wagon train's appearance passed quickly around the circle. Soon they could see it slowly wending its way down a distant hill. Many went out to meet it. Those who remained behind waited in feverish eagerness for any news the newcomers might bring.

When the smaller train finally arrived and made camp near the Blake group, Missie and Willie soon discovered the second train had begun its journey far south of their own area, and they had to be satisfied with only general news. The wagon master turned out to be a good deal more impatient than their Mr. Blake. After sitting downriver for only two days, he decided that the water had receded enough for him to get his wagons across. Mr. Blake tried to dissuade him, but the man laughed it off, roughly declaring Blake to be as skitterish as an old woman. He had taken wagons across when the water had been even higher, he stoutly and loudly maintained. He then turned to the waiting wagons and ordered the first one into the water.

Women and children joined the men on the bank to watch the wagons cross. Murmured complaints about Mr. Blake passed among the observers. "Here we been sittin' when we coulda been days away from here" was muttered around the group.

Mr. Blake did not choose to watch. With a look of disgust

and a few well-chosen words directed at the other wagon master, he spun on his heel and marched off.

It seemed for a time that all would go well with the wagon. Then, to the horror of all those on the bank, it suddenly hit the deeper water and the current lifted it up and swirled it about. The horses plunged and fought in their effort to swim for the distant shore, but the churning waters were too strong for them. When the driver realized his predicament, he threw himself into the murky deep, trying desperately to fight his way to the shore. The wagon, weaving and swaying, was swept downstream as the frantic horses neighed and struggled in their fright. The pitching canvas cover gave one last sickening heave and then toppled over on its side. The sinking wagon and team were carried downstream and out of sight around a bend in the river.

Meantime, the driver was fighting to keep his head above water. At one point he managed to grab a floating tree that was also being carried along by the muddy current. A cheer went up from the shore, but the next instant a groan passed through the entire group—the tree struck something under the surface and flipped in midstream, jarring the man loose and leaving him to struggle on his own again.

The riverbank became alive with activity as men scrambled for their horses in an effort to reach near enough to at least throw him a rope. The observers watched the bobbing spot of his dark head as the water swirled him around the river bend. A young woman in the group from the other train collapsed in a heap, and some of the women who traveled with her bent over her to give her assistance.

"Poor woman," Missie gasped. "It must be her man!" She covered her face with her hands and wept.

The body was pulled from the river about a half mile downstream. All attempts to force some life back into the man were futile. The horses and wagon were never seen again.

The following day the travelers from both wagon trains met together. The grave had been dug and a service was held for the drowned man. His widow had to be helped away from the heaped-up mound that held the body of her young husband. A feeling of helplessness and grief settled over both camps. Respect for Mr. Blake mounted, and most of the group averted their eyes when the other wagon master, looking rather subdued, passed by.

A new determination passed through the Blake train. They would wait. They would wait if it took all summer! Horse and wagon were no match for the angry waters.

After breakfast one day a week later, someone in the camp drew their attention to a hill across the river. On ponies, their faces painted and headdress feathers waving in the wind, sat several Indian braves. The almost-naked bodies glistened in the morning sun. In silence they gazed across the river at the ring of wagons. Then at a signal from their leader, they moved on and out of sight over the hill. Missie shivered as she wondered what could have happened if the churning water had not been between them. Maybe this was a fulfillment of the Scripture promise she and Willie had been given by her father before they left home, "Yea, I will help thee. . . ."

After another week of patient and not-so-patient waiting, the river finally did recede. Mr. Blake, who had been carefully watching it each day, crossed it on his horse before he allowed any wagon to put a wheel into the water. When he felt satisfied, the order was given to move out.

It took the whole day to make the crossing. The women and children were guided across on horseback to await the coming of their menfolk and the canvas-covered homes. Some of the wagons needed two teams in order to pull them across. Many outriders traveled beside each wagon, steadying it with the many ropes that Mr. Blake insisted upon; thus no wagon got caught in midstream by a current that tried to take it sideways rather than forward. Missie couldn't help but remember the tragic death in the other group. If the other wagon master had used such precautions . . . Mr. Blake was a careful and experienced wagon master—another of God's provisions.

Once the group was gathered on the river's western shore, Willie offered a prayer of thanks to God for all the travelers. The weary men and animals were glad to make camp once more for a good night's rest before taking to the trail. The next day they would resume their journey after their month-and-a-half delay.

Missie was becoming increasingly concerned about Becky. They still had many days on the trail before reaching Tettsford Junction. Would Mrs. Kosensky's midwifery services be required after all?

———

Early the next morning the camp was a bustle of activity. The travelers could hardly wait for the word to move out. Even the horses stamped in their impatience. Missie was surprised at the feelings that clamored for attention within her. During their previous weeks on the trail, she had dreaded the crossing of the Big River, for it seemed to mark the point of no return. But now that it was finally behind them, she was as restless as the teams. She felt like starting out to walk on her own. If she had known the trail and the direction she was to take, she might have done just that.

Finally the wagons were lined up and the order shouted. The creak of the harnesses and grind of wheels sounded like music to Missie's ears. At last! They were on their way again! All were alive and accounted for. They had crossed the Big River; surely only lesser obstacles lay in their pathway. Since turning back was no longer possible, she was anxious to forge ahead.

Missie could sense Willie's excitement as he carefully guided the team to follow the wagon ahead of him. It was hard for him to restrain himself from urging them on at a faster speed, but no one in the long line of teams was allowed to change the pace set by the wagon master.

The day passed uneventfully. The travelers quickly fell into their familiar routines. But their aching muscles reminded them that they had been idle for too long and must again break in to the rigors of the trail. Missie walked and rode in turn, gathering sticks as she walked, and when she climbed up again to ride, she stashed her bundle under the wagon seat.

At day's end everyone was weary, but tensions were gone. They were moving again, and that was what mattered.

———

As they progressed, the land about them continued its gradual change. There were fewer trees now, and those that did grow were smaller than the ones left behind. The women found very little wood for their fires as they followed the train. They began to carry buckets, which they filled with buffalo chips. Missie had preferred the wood, which made a much more pleasant fire. Besides, the cumbersome buckets soon had one's arms and back aching.

Occasionally herds of buffalo or deer were seen off in the distance. Twice, Indians were sighted, but though the hearts of the travelers beat more rapidly for a time, these Indians did not approach the train.

The widow of the drowned man, Mrs. Emory, had asked Mr. Blake for permission to join his train. Mr. Blake had found it impossible to refuse her. Arrangements were made for her to share Mr. Weiss's wagon with his daughter, Kathy. Mr. Weiss moved in with Henry, and the train moved on.

The unfortunate woman had lost everything in the river—her husband of six months, her home, and her belongings. The women of similar size dug into their trunks and showered her with enough garments to outfit her for the remainder of the trip to Tettsford Junction. Though some of the clothes didn't fit very well and weren't particularly fashionable, Mrs. Emory was very grateful for their kindness.

She proved to be a worthy member of the train. Even in her deep sorrow, she was aware of those about her who could use her helping hand. Her quiet manner and helpful acts won her a secure place in the group.

And so they journeyed on. Each day found them a little nearer to their respective destinations, and talk around the fire at night was filled with shared hopes and plans and dreams. The new land held many promises. It seemed to hold out open arms, ready to embrace a stranger—any stranger with hope in his heart and a strong back willing to bend itself to the work.

NINE

Town

Mr. Blake seemed to have a great aversion to towns. In every possible instance, he skirted far around them, no matter how small the settlement. When he could not avoid one, he ordered the wagons to keep on moving. No one was allowed to stop for any dallying. Each family made a list of needed supplies, and either Mr. Blake or one of his scouts rode into the town and made the purchases.

The wagon master said his job was to get the wagons, and the folks in them, to Tettsford Junction, and he planned to do just that. Further, he said the most deadly enemy of the westbound settler was a town. Blake had lost no one to swollen rivers, prairie fires, or Indians on his many trains west. But he had lost people to *towns,* he grumbled. And since he did not like having his good record smudged, he considered towns the enemy.

Everyone was surprised, therefore, when Mr. Blake called a meeting and announced, "Tomorrow we reach Lipton. Ain't much of a town, but we'll be stopping there fer a day. Our campsite is to the right of the town within easy walking distance. No teams—no horses a'tall, no wagons—are to go into the town. Those of you thet have more purchases to make than can be carried will be glad to know the Lipton General Store will make deliveries. The place carries a fair line of essentials."

He stopped a moment to look around the circle.

"The train will move on again at the usual hour on Wednesday mornin'. I suggest ya all be ready to go."

A general uproar of excitement followed his announcement. To see a town again! To be able to more than just drive by, only imagining the opportunity of browsing through shops, going to the barber, selecting food delicacies . . .

How large was the town? Did it have a blacksmith? A hairdresser? A butcher? Maybe even a doctor? Questions flew furiously, but Blake was the only one with answers—and he had somehow disappeared after his announcement.

Missie couldn't help smiling as she and Willie walked back to their wagon. Her mind was busy calculating just what she wanted most and whether they would be able to spare any of their hard-earned cash in order to purchase it.

It was difficult to break from their fire that night and get to bed. Missie delved into a trunk to pull out a favorite dress. Shaking out the wrinkles as best she could, she hung the blue-flowered frock up in hopes it would be smooth by morning. She had noticed some wives adding another patch to their husband's already worn overalls. Whole families pored over lists, adding, changing, dreaming, wishing—and reluctantly deleting.

Missie thought even the dogs of the camp had seemed to catch the fever. They ran back and forth, yapping and tussling and making general nuisances of themselves.

The next morning everyone was ready to roll long before the call was given—even the often tardy Standards. The sooner they began the journey, the sooner Lipton would be reached—and the longer the time available for shopping.

The wagons lumbered out, set for another dusty day on the trail, everyone hoping that it wouldn't be too late when they made camp to be off to the town.

To everyone's amazement and delight, the town lay before

them as they topped the first hill. They had camped only a few miles from it the night before! They all laughed at themselves and at their wagon master, but Mr. Blake's face remained as impassive as ever.

They quickly reached the new campsite and formed their customary circle. The men set about the task of caring for the animals while the women scurried around, building fires to heat water for sponge baths within the confines of their wagons. By the time they and their children were ready to head into town, the sun had climbed high into the clear sky for another extremely warm day.

They departed in little groups, eager and expectant. Henry accompanied some of the younger people. The Collinses walked together, Sissie with Meggie in her arms and Tom with Joey hoisted on his shoulders. Mrs. Thorne strode off, her offspring matching her long strides. Her husband grumbled that he would have none of the foolishness and elected to stay behind and mend the harness. Mrs. Page, after voicing a parting barb at Jessie Tuttle, hurried down the trail without even waiting for a reply. Tillie Crane went along, too impatient to wait even for her young husband. At last she could have *something* done to her hair! Mrs. Schmidt threw a bundle of hastily gathered sticks under the protection of her wagon, shook out her apron, and started off with her family members. They quickly overtook and passed the slow-moving Mrs. Kosensky.

Missie and Willie walked with John and Becky. They chose a much slower pace for Becky's sake.

As they passed the Weiss' wagon, they saw Mrs. Emory fastening the tent flap down before leaving for town. Her sad face lit up with a smile when she saw the young couples. Without a word, Willie stepped over to lend her a hand.

"Eager to git into town?" She directed her question to the women.

"Oh yes," Becky enthused. "It seems like forever since I've walked on a boardwalk or looked in a shop."

Mrs. Emory just smiled.

She is so attractive when she smiles like that, thought Missie, *and so very young. I reckon she's not much older than I am. What would I do if something happened to my Willie? How would I ever get home again? Would I just be stranded somewhere out here in the West?* Just the thought of such a thing made Missie's stomach churn. *Dear God,* she prayed inwardly, *I don't think I could stand it.*

Then she thought of her own mother. A new awareness of what Marty had been through those long years before filled her being, and tears threatened to fill her eyes. She hurriedly blinked them away before anyone could notice them.

"Are you going shopping, too?" she asked Mrs. Emory.

The woman's face sobered, and she shook her head. "Not exactly," she replied slowly.

Missie realized the woman would probably have nothing to go shopping with, even though her needs were great.

There was silence for a minute. The young woman seemed to be debating whether she should say anything further about her plans for the day. Finally she spoke, her voice soft and even. "I . . . I'm really goin' to look for a church. I . . . have this need for a place of prayer."

Willie reached for the woman's hand. He just looked into her face and patted the small hand with his other one. Missie blinked back more tears. The woman nodded, withdrew her hand, and turned away with tears glistening on her cheeks.

Missie then reached for Willie's hand. He was so much like her pa, her Willie. He felt so deeply what others were feeling. Homesickness for her father and a surge of love for Willie swept through Missie in one wave.

They followed the Clays, who were already walking slowly down the path toward town.

"Willie," Missie whispered, "we should try to draw her out more. She's such a sweet thing, the poor soul. I can't imagine anyone suffering so much—so young."

"Yer ma an' pa did," Willie reminded her gently. His hand tightened on hers.

Missie was silent, too deeply moved to try to speak. Yes, her ma and pa had suffered, but she had been too young to be aware of it. She only remembered them as laughing, loving parents. Would Mrs. Emory someday be able to laugh and love again, too? Missie prayed that the town would indeed have a fine little church where she could commune with God.

The town wasn't much, as towns go, but to the travelers it would suffice. There were sidewalks for Becky to walk on, although there were loose, broken, and even missing boards. The shoppers soon learned to keep an eye on their next step.

After a quick general look at the town, the various couples separated. The women went to yearn over threads, yarn, yard goods, and other "luxuries." The men found themselves around the livery stable to check on more "practical" supplies, such as a new harness or new shoes for the horses.

Becky and Missie spent a long part of their morning surveying soft yarns and materials, planning and dreaming of what they would make for their coming babies. Becky already had most of her necessities, her baby having been expected before she left home, but she was eager to add some special things to the baby's wardrobe. Missie would wait for her main preparation until she reached Willie's land and was settled—but it would be so much fun to select a few pieces to work on during the journey.

There was a hotel of sorts in Lipton, and Becky's and Missie's husbands had promised to take their wives there for a meal. The four looked forward to it eagerly. It would be so good to have food that didn't taste of woodsmoke, to drink real store-bought tea, to eat meat that wasn't wild, and maybe even have some fresh bread. And vegetables! How long it had been since they had tasted fresh vegetables!

Promptly at noon the men returned and made an elaborate display of escorting Missie and Becky to the dining room. The room was already crowded, and they had to wait for a table.

The two couples deliberated long over the menu, and finally, sensing the impatience of the waitress, placed their orders. Missie was surprised at how flat things tasted without the tang of the smoke. The bread turned out not to be fresh, but it *was* bread. The meat was mild enough, but more than a little tough, and the vegetables were definitely overcooked. They enjoyed it immensely, however, and pretended to one another that it was the finest they had ever eaten. They even ordered pie and lingered over it, savoring each bite as they slowly sipped their cups of tea.

In the afternoon they continued their inspection of the stores. They knew wise decisions had to be made, and each purchase had to be carefully considered. It was a difficult task to make up one's mind after not having shopped for such a long time.

Their lists were consulted and changed before the goods were finally ordered. Necessary foods were restocked, and a few fresh vegetables were purchased. Missie did pick out a few soft flannels and cottons to make into baby clothes and also bought additional wool for heavy socks. They began their walk back, weary and a little poorer, but refreshed by their day spent back in civilization. They clutched in their arms a few of their most cherished purchases, eagerly awaiting the rest to be delivered that evening.

Missie and Willie left John and Becky at their wagon and

walked on to their own. Becky was looking tired after her exciting and busy day—this in spite of the fact that Missie had insisted she sit and rest for a spell every so often throughout the time spent in town. Missie invited them to share the evening meal with them so Becky might get some much-needed rest. Becky was happy to accept.

Upon reaching the wagon, Missie stowed away her purchases and set to work building the fire and preparing the meal. Willie changed back into his old overalls and went to take care of the cows and horses.

It had been a good day. Missie hummed as she worked. She could hear Willie's whistle moving down the path toward the draw where the animals were staked out to graze.

TEN

Breaking Camp

The town, as Mr. Blake feared, had produced some casualties. Tillie Crane had found her hairdresser. She had also found a job in a shop, and she adamantly refused to move one more step into that "God-forsaken land" of wind, sun, and rain. Her husband had spent the night badgering and pleading by turn, but nothing would make Tillie change her mind. A heartbroken Jason Crane finally came to inform Mr. Blake that their wagon would be withdrawing. There was no way he would travel on without his wife. He'd see what he could do for a job in Lipton. Surely there was work somewhere for a man who was willing.

The Cranes weren't the only ones with problems. A number of the men from the train had been "out on the town." Most of them staggered in, sometime during the night, in various stages of disrepair. Mrs. Kosensky had taken care of her husband—a cold bucket of water for the outside of him and several cups of hot coffee for his insides. The next morning he was bleary-eyed and a bit belligerent but ready for travel.

Jessie Tuttle handled her driver-brother, J. M. Dooley, by simply stuffing him into the wagon and hitching the team herself.

Mrs. Thorne had the most trouble. Her husband failed to reappear at all. After waiting tight-lipped, she set off for town in search of her errant man, striding back to camp empty-handed after two hours of searching. It was Mr. Blake's turn. Maybe he was more familiar with where to look; at any rate, after about three-quarters of an hour, he returned. The livery wagon followed, delivering a very sodden Mr. Thorne. His wife said nothing, simply nodding to the men where Mr. Thorne was to be placed and picking up the reins of her team.

After a three-hour delay, the teams finally moved out. By then the sun was already hot, the children cranky, and the adults out of sorts.

Mrs. Thorne did not so much as give her neighbors a nod or a suggestion of apology. She smacked her team smartly with a rein and maneuvered into position, her face stern and her eyes straight ahead.

Missie watched as the woman drove up in her wagon. It had been said that Mrs. Thorne had known all along her husband wouldn't remain in the camp mending harnesses and that she knew exactly what he would do once he got to town. It had happened many times in the past and would likely happen often in the future.

Missie was sure the invincible Mrs. Thorne would be able to cope. Nothing seemed to shake that woman from solid-rock indifference.

Mrs. Thorne smacked her team again and passed on by, her hands steady, her eyes unblinking against the glare of the mid-morning sun. Missie almost missed it, but there it was—and what she saw made her stop short and catch her breath. Unmistakably running down Mrs. Thorne's coarse, tanned cheeks was a steady stream of tears.

When Missie could breathe again she whispered, "You poor soul. Here you are suffering inside, and nobody knows . . . nobody even suspects, so no one reaches out to you in understanding. Oh . . . God forgive me. Forgive me for not seeing past her stiff jaw to the hurts and needs. Help me to help her, Lord—to show her kindness and love. She needs me. She needs *you*, Lord."

Thereafter, Missie took every opportunity she could find to greet the woman with a smile, to show little acts of kindness. The older woman did not really melt, but she did begin to show a little softness around the firm, hard edges of her soul.

———

They had been on the trail four days since leaving Lipton, and the wagon train seemed to be making good progress. The men who had visited the tavern had sobered up and were now back to their hard tasks. But it was strongly suspected J. M. Dooley had somehow managed to smuggle some whiskey along in his wagon against Mr. Blake's explicit orders. It was a true source of contention between J. M. and Jessie Tuttle. And, of course, anything involving Jessie, Mrs. Page considered her right to become involved in, as well. So a three-way war was now raging.

Folks smiled at the ridiculousness of it all, but finally Mr. Blake decided it was time to step in. J. M.'s booze was discovered and discarded. Mrs. Page and her wagon were assigned a new position at the end of the line far from Jessie Tuttle. Things seemed to settle down again.

———

When they made camp the fourth night, a message carried by Mrs. Kosensky's daughter, Nell, arrived for Missie as she cleaned up after the evening meal.

"Ma says, could ya come to Mrs. Clay? She's been in labor most of the afternoon an' wants to see ya."

Missie was stunned at the news. She had missed Becky that day but had supposed she just didn't feel up to taking in her customary short walks alongside the train. Missie called over to Henry to tell Willie where she would be and quickly grabbed a shawl. In her haste she almost ran to get to Becky but held herself back lest others watching would be unduly concerned.

As she approached the Clay wagon she could hear Becky's soft moaning. She ran the last few steps and was met by a very worried-looking Mrs. Kosensky. Instead of inviting Missie up, the other woman climbed down and drew Missie aside.

"Ain't good, ma'am, ain't good," she said in a hoarse whisper. "Me . . . I deliver babies. Yes, lotsa babies . . . but this kind, no. He small . . . he twisted . . . and he early." She shook her head, and Missie noticed tears in her eyes. "Ain't good. She need a doctor . . . bad."

"May I see her?" Missie begged, longing to be a source of comfort and aid to Becky.

"Yes . . . yes, do."

Missie scrambled up into the wagon. Becky was flushed and damp with perspiration. Missie looked at her pale, anguished face in alarm. She reached for Becky's hand and then began to smooth back her long, loose hair. She spoke softly, not really aware of what she said to Becky, but it seemed to comfort the distraught girl.

Missie stayed with Becky for most of the night, but the situation did not improve. Occasionally, Becky seemed to drift off into a troubled sleep, but she was soon reawakened by her discomfort. Willie, who had come to wait outside by the fire with John, suggested that Missie should get some rest or she would be in danger, too. Mrs. Kosensky agreed.

The next morning the LaHayes crawled wearily from their bed and began the preparations for another day on the trail. Missie sent Willie over to ask about Becky. He returned with the news that nothing had changed. Missie's heart felt heavy as she went through the motions of preparing their breakfast.

While she was hurrying to pack up their belongings, one of the trail scouts came by on his horse. He stopped at each wagon with the same message.

"Mr. Blake says we stay put today. He's not breakin' camp till thet baby's arrived."

Missie was greatly relieved and would have willingly hugged the grisly wagon master. She could not imagine what it would be like for Becky if she had to bounce around in a moving wagon in her condition.

A rider had been sent back to Lipton the night before to see if a doctor could be found and brought to the camp. Everyone who knew how, and even some who didn't, prayed that there might be a doctor and that he would arrive soon.

The women tried to keep busy with a little cleaning and straightening up of their wagon homes, and men checked harnesses and wheels. Neighbors used the long hours as an excuse to sit and discuss anything that came to mind. Still the time only crawled, and by the time the day was coming to an end, everyone's nerves were on edge. Becky and her unborn baby were a heavy concern on everyone's mind.

With no more valid reason to stay up, they finally extinguished their campfires and went to bed, hoping that the good news of the baby's birth would reach them during the night.

It did not happen.

As they stirred about the camp the next morning, the news spread quickly that the child had not yet been born. Another long day began. With no harnesses to mend and no further wagon cleaning to be done, time lay heavy on hands and minds. Yet hope remained alive. Surely with the additional delay, the doctor from Lipton would have plenty of time to make it. But the rider finally returned, tired and dusty and with a weary, limping horse. There was no doctor to be found in Lipton.

It was almost one-thirty in the afternoon when Mrs.

Kosensky climbed down from the Clay wagon. Willie, Missie, and several other neighbors had been waiting outside. No cry of a newborn baby followed her. Mrs. Kosensky's shoulders sagged and tears coursed down her plump cheeks. To the waiting friends she shook her head.

"No," she said brokenly. "No . . . he did not make it, the little one."

"Oh, Becky!" cried Missie. "Poor Becky. She'll be heartbroken."

"No," said Mrs. Kosensky, again shaking her head. "No. The little mama . . . she did not make it, either."

For a moment Missie chose not to understand, not to believe. But she knew, as she looked at the older woman, that the news was indeed true. Then, from the depths of the covered wagon, came muffled sobs of a man.

"Oh, dear God," Missie whispered with her hands to her face. She didn't know if her legs could hold her upright. Willie was by her side in a moment, and she turned to bury her face against his shoulder. He held her close for a time and let her weep. When her spasm of tears had subsided, he gently held her away and looked into her face.

"I must go in to John," he said. "Can you make it to the wagon alone?"

Missie nodded, but it was Henry who led her away, easing her over the rough terrain and opening the canvas flap so she could stumble into the wagon.

She lay down in the stuffy heat and once more felt overcome with the sorrow and confusion in her soul.

The funeral service was held the next morning. John stood in bewildered silence as the young mother and her infant son were laid together in a blanket. Shock and grief no doubt had numbed his mind, and he didn't seem to comprehend the event.

After the service was over, the wagons were quietly ordered to move out. The men guided their animals into line silently, thoughtfully. Willie had suggested that John ride with them for a while, but he preferred to be alone. Missie rode beside Willie, but they had not gone far before she asked if he would stop a moment so she could climb down and walk for a while.

She stood quietly for a time, letting the wagons roll past her, turning her back to the dust swirling from their wheels. When the last one had gone by, Missie looked back the way they had come. In the valley below was the circle where they had camped. The evidence of a recent train was still there—the trampled grass, the campfire ashes, the wheel marks—and there, just to the left, was the little mound of bare earth marking the spot where they had left Becky. And Becky's baby. For a moment Missie wanted to run back, but she knew it was pointless. Becky was gone from them now. Missie felt a certain measure of comfort in the thought that Becky and her baby were not alone. They had each other.

"Good-bye, Becky," Missie whispered. "Good-bye, Rebecca Clay. You were a dear, sweet friend. May you—and your little one—find great pleasure and comfort in the house of God."

Missie turned to go, tears streaming down her face. But just then a lone rider emerged from the bushes in the valley and stopped beside the soft mound. Missie recognized the form of Mr. Blake. The man dismounted from his horse and approached the new grave. He removed his hat and stood momentarily with bowed head. Then he bent down and placed a small cluster of prairie flowers on the fresh earth. As he turned and mounted his horse, Missie felt a fresh stream of tears slide down her cheeks.

That was a lovely thing to do, she thought.

But it was much later that Missie learned that many years

before, the same man had stood beside another mound—one that held his own wife and infant son. At that time, too, he had been forced to ride away and leave them to lie alone beside a prairie trail.

ELEVEN

A Tough Decision

Missie found a measure of comfort in the fact that Tettsford Junction was getting nearer and nearer, but the days always seemed long. She kept herself occupied as much as she could. She carefully looked after her own responsibilities, as well as devoting much time to helping others—especially Mrs. Collins. The two Collins youngsters kept quite healthy, in spite of the rigors of the trail. But they were young enough to still require a lot of time and attention.

Missie and Willie had not yet been able to talk about Becky's death. Missie wept often. If Willie was there when she cried, he held her close, stroking her hair and listening to her sorrow with his heart. They each realized that sometime—and sometime soon—they must discuss it. Probably only then could their hearts begin the true healing process.

John Clay's name was always mentioned in Willie's evening prayer. But though Missie ached for John and his loss, she also realized she felt a twinge of resentment toward him. Her emotions swung between grief and anger.

One night, after they had retired, Willie gently broached the subject they had been avoiding.

"It easin' some—'bout Becky?" His arm tightened around Missie as he asked the question. She could tell he wanted her to know that he understood, that he suffered with her.

"I guess . . . some," Missie was able to answer, holding back the tears.

"I think maybe it's gittin' harder for John," Willie commented after a few moments of silence.

"How so?"

"Well, at first I don't think it . . . it was real to John. Now it is. He's over the shock. An' he's missin' Becky . . . knowin' thet she won't be back, won't be his . . . ever again."

Missie pondered Willie's words. That small feeling of anger toward John stirred within her. She decided to express it.

"John was too sure of himself, too cocky about Becky and that baby. Just because his mother . . . Things can go wrong . . . they can. He should have known that." Now Missie could no longer hold back her tears.

"I was feelin' those same thoughts," Willie said quietly, "but maybe we're bein' too hard on John. Sure, he was cocky. But . . . but maybe it was just a cover-up, to sorta make things happen the way he wanted them to. I don't know. All I know is thet he loved Becky . . . very much . . . an' he wanted thet son . . . very much. An' now he has neither of them . . . an' he's truly sorrowin', Missie. Maybe . . . maybe we're *all* guilty of holdin' too lightly those we love."

Missie's sobs quieted as she thought over Willie's words. He was right, of course. John did love Becky, and he had wanted the baby. It was no fault of John's that things had gone wrong. If it hadn't been for the long delay at the Big River, they would have reached Tettsford Junction and the doctor in time—even with Becky's baby arriving early.

A feeling of great sorrow for John swept over Missie. *The poor man . . . to lose so much.* She must pray for him more, she decided.

Willie interrupted her thoughts. "Missie . . ."

When he didn't continue, she turned toward him, but it

was too dark in the wagon to read his face.

"I been thinkin'," he finally said, his voice low but determined. "When we git to Tettsford Junction, there's a doc there."

"I know."

"I want ya to have a doc, Missie."

"But our baby is almost three months away," she said.

"I know."

Missie thought about it. "I suppose we could," she finally stated, "get back to Tettsford Junction in time. How far is our land from Tettsford Junction?"

"Good week's travel by wagon."

"A week? I suppose if we left early enough—"

"That's not what I had in mind, Missie," Willie said too quickly.

"What *did* you have in mind?"

Willie swallowed. "Well, I figured thet maybe ya should stay at Tettsford until after the baby is safely delivered."

"But you're in a great hurry to get to the land—to put up some corrals, fix a house, and get yourself some cattle before winter."

"Yeah, yer right, Missie, but—"

"That'd make you late and rushed. By the time I'm ready to travel and we make the trip, you'd hardly have time—"

Willie interrupted. "I'd go on as planned, Missie, an' see to all those things."

"An' leave me behind?" Missie could scarcely believe her ears.

"It's the only way, Missie . . . far as I can see."

"But I don't want—"

Willie's arm tightened again, but his voice was firm. "I don't want it, either, Missie, but it's the only way. I'm not takin' any chances like John took. I will not—"

But Missie quickly stopped him. "It's not the same . . . can't you see? Becky was sick from the beginning. Me . . . I've been fine all along."

Missie felt Willie's hand grip her shoulder.

"It *could happen* thet ya need a doctor. There are no doctors where we're goin'. There aren't even neighbors who could be midwives. There's no one to help ya, Missie. No one! Can't ya see? I can't take ya there. Not after what's happened here!"

A sob caught in Missie's throat, but she tried one more time. "Then we'll just have to go back to Tettsford when the time comes. I don't want to stay there without you, Willie. We'll just have to go back."

"An' iffen the baby comes early—like Becky's? How will we know when it's time? Something could go wrong *anytime*. Already I'm prayin' every night thet you'll be fine fer the next day's travel, fine till we reach Tettsford. Iffen I take ya on from there, down to the ranch with the idea of bringin' ya back— what iffen we're caught on the trail? What then?"

Missie knew she had lost, for the moment. She didn't bother to argue anymore but buried her face against Willie's shoulder and wept. To be without Willie for three long months or more, in a strange town, waiting all alone for their first baby . . . how could she ever bear it?

She felt a tear drop onto her forehead. Willie was weeping, too.

"It's gonna be so hard," he finally managed to say, his voice husky. "So awful hard . . . but we'll make it. Remember our verse—'Fear thou not; for I am with thee: be not dismayed; for I am thy God: I will strengthen thee; yea, I will help thee; yea, I will uphold thee with the right hand of my righteousness'!"

Fear thou not echoed over and over through Missie's mind. How could she *not* be afraid?

———

The wagon train made its final camp just outside Tettsford Junction. The town proved to be a larger settlement than anyone on the train had anticipated. Missie looked around at the bleakness of the countryside and wondered what sustained it. The land about didn't appear able to produce any more than a bit of sagebrush. *Who could possibly endure such barrenness?* Missie thought with a shiver. She turned her back on the wind that seemed to be constantly blowing.

The traveling companions from the many weeks shared mixed emotions. John still felt empty and alone. He had difficulty deciding what he should do, whether to continue on his way and join his brother as planned or look for some kind of work in the town. The bright promises that the land had held for him seemed empty now that Becky was gone.

The Pages made up their minds to stay in town, as did a couple of other families that Missie didn't know very well. Jessie Tuttle would continue on, so Mrs. Page saved a few choice sentences for a parting shot. Jessie ignored the needling, much to Mrs. Page's annoyance and everyone else's amusement.

Mrs. Emory, the young widow, knew she had very few options open to her. She would stay in the town. The kindness of the members of the wagon train had gotten her to Tettsford Junction. Now it was up to her to take care of herself. She had blossomed and matured during her days on the trail, and though she still obviously felt the loss of her husband, she seemed prepared to face life again.

Mr. Weiss and Kathy also decided to remain in Tettsford. Her father declared with certainty that such a busy town would be able to use another smithy. Missie wondered if that was the real reason—or if he had developed a secret attachment to the young widow and was willing to bide his time. She rather hoped not. Melinda Emory was scarcely older than Mr. Weiss's daughter, Kathy. But it was their business, Missie decided, and

Mr. Weiss certainly was a very kind man.

Most of the other travelers would be leaving in a few days' time with other trains, traveling northwest to the "prairies." Missie couldn't see how any place could be more *prairie* than where they were at present, and how anyone would actually *choose* to live here. But she did not voice her opinions.

Willie asked Missie if she wanted to go in and see the town as soon as camp was made and the necessary tasks performed. But she was remembering her last visit to town in the company of Becky and was thinking ahead to her own dreaded stay in this one.

She declined and excused herself to the wagon to be alone.

If only Willie would change his mind! Did he expect her to spend three miserable months cooped up in this horribly cramped wagon? In this dreary town, with the sun beating relentlessly on the treeless landscape and the wind howling constantly about the canvas flaps? If only she had known ahead of time that Willie wouldn't be taking her on to his land, to help build a home and establish his ranch. She might as well have stayed at home with her own folks who loved her and would have provided for her. *Why trek halfway across the world and suffer all of the heat, the rain, the mosquitoes, the blistered and aching feet— just to be dumped off here?* Her thoughts raged round and round in her mind. It just wasn't fair of Willie. It wasn't fair at all.

The hot tears coursed down her face, and Missie finally fell into an exhausted sleep.

Willie started calling to Missie even before he entered the wagon. "I've found a place!" she heard him call, obviously elated. Missie quickly sat up.

"A place for *what*?" she demanded when his head poked through the canvas flap.

"For you," he declared, looking surprised at her question. "For you—while yer waitin'."

She stared at him. So Willie hadn't ever planned for her to spend these months waiting in the wagon.

Missie stubbornly didn't tell him she didn't intend to *wait*. She intended to *go*. But deep inside she knew it was useless to fight it.

"It's only one room—but it's a nice fair size. An' it's with fine folks. I'm sure you'll like 'em, an' they even said I can stay there, too, till the supply train is ready to leave."

"That's right good of them," Missie said with some spark, "seeing how you *are* my husband."

Willie ignored the remark. "Mr. Taylorson runs a general store, an' his wife teaches a bit of piano. Says ya might even learn to play the piano while yer waitin'."

"Oh, Willie!" Missie said in exasperation. "What in heaven's name would I want to learn piano for? What good would that do me where—"

"It would help fill in the long hours," Willie interposed. "It might help a heap, iffen ya choose to let it." His tone was mild, but he gave her a searching look.

Missie wanted to stomp away, but there was no place to go—neighbors' eyes were watching all around. So she turned her back on Willie and began to trim the wick of the lantern that usually sat on the outside shelf, making sure she seemed at ease and composed.

Willie continued, "The doc lives only three houses down from the Taylorsons, so he'll be right handy when—"

"If he's not off somewhere setting a broken leg or treating a bullet wound," Missie muttered.

"Guess thet could happen even back home," Willie said calmly. "But there are two midwives in town—in case he should be away. I inquired."

"Midwife didn't help Becky none."

Missie grimaced at her own unreasonableness. She was

being unfair to Willie. She knew that. He was doing what he believed was right. She blinked back her tears and steadied her voice.

"An' when does the supply train go?" she asked, deliberately changing the course of the conversation.

"'Bout a week—maybe a little less."

"And you'll be ready?"

"Plan to be. Think I'll do like yer pa suggested. I'll pick me up another wagon with the rails fer the corrals an' other supplies. That way, I won't be held up none once I git to our land."

"And where would this treeless town ever get rails for a corral?" Missie couldn't keep her dislike for the place from her voice.

"They haul 'em in. Lots of folks need 'em. Guess there's lumber a lot closer than it looks—some of those hills to the west are treed."

Missie nodded bleakly.

"Well, I'd best see to the stock," Willie said and turned to go, then turned back again. "Henry said to let ya know he won't be here fer supper."

"What's he planning?"

"He's eatin' with the Weisses. But what he's *plannin'*—who knows?"

Missie smiled in spite of herself. So it was Kathy Weiss that Henry was setting his cap for. He had kept her guessing the whole trip, seeming to give equal attention to more than one girl. Well, at least Kathy also would be staying on in Tettsford— Missie would be assured of some company.

As she began work on the evening meal, she regretted her refusal to go into town. She could have been cooking something special and fresh for supper instead of the same old fare— if she hadn't chosen to remain at the wagon feeling mistreated and sorry for herself.

She was bored with the food, she was bored with the wagon, she was even bored with her neighbors. Tomorrow she *would* go into town. She might even let Willie introduce her to the Taylorsons. It wasn't their fault she would be stuck here in the town until the baby arrived. Not their fault at all.

TWELVE

The Taylorsons

Missie awoke refreshed and ready to venture into Tettsford Junction. She determined to make the best of the day. She washed carefully and chose one of her favorite dresses. Loose and full, with a sash that tied in the back, the small print was cheerful and becoming. Missie was relieved it would be usable throughout her confinement—though it wouldn't be as stylish as when it showed off her slim waist. The loose shirtwaists and expandable skirts she and her mama had prepared for "some future day" when Missie would be needing them were suitable for everyday wear. But Missie was not too taken with the plain, simple dark skirts and was thankful she had a nice assortment of colorful aprons to wear over them. She combed her hair with particular care and began to prepare breakfast for the men.

Henry was the first to appear. He seemed to approve of how Missie looked.

"See yer not wearin' yer hikin' shoes today," he joked.

Missie looked down at her trim feet carefully encased in smart black boots. She smiled.

"I just may *never* wear them again," she answered in kind.

"Now, now," Henry replied, "ya sure wouldn't want thet part of yer edjication to jest go to waste, would ya?"

"Seems every *other* part of my education has gone to waste," Missie responded. There was a little quiver in her voice as she thought of the classroom of eager children back home.

"Not so," Henry was quick to say. "Don't fergit thet you'll soon be 'teacher' agin."

Missie glanced down at her blossoming figure and felt her cheeks grow warm.

Henry quickly changed the subject. "See'd the town yet?"

"Not yet—but Willie has. I didn't feel much like going in yesterday. I'm more ready today."

Henry nodded. "Big place really—but not too fancy."

"Where do you think they got the name?"

"Man named Tettsford first set up a store there to catch the trade of the wagons goin' through."

"Is he still there?"

"Naw. He made his money, then cleared out. Went back east—to spend it, I guess."

"Smart man," Missie murmured under her breath.

"Ya know what I'm gonna miss most 'bout wagon trainin'?" Henry asked.

His abrupt change of subject surprised Missie, but she soon recovered and answered with a teasing voice, "Now, I *wonder*."

Henry turned red. "Naw," he said, "nothin' like thet. I'm gonna miss the Sunday gatherin's."

Missie quickly turned serious. "I guess I will, too," she said. "They weren't anything like home, but they were special in their own way, weren't they? And you did a first-rate job, Henry. A very good job. Did you ever think of being a preacher?"

Henry's color deepened. "I thought on it . . . sorta. But I ain't got what it takes to be a preacher. Very little book learnin' and not much civilizin', either."

"That's not true, Henry," Missie remonstrated with him. "You're a born leader. Didn't you notice how the people followed you, accepted you, expected you to take the lead?"

Henry sat silently. "They did, some," he agreed. "But thet was a wagon train, not a settlement church. There's a heap of difference there. I did decide one thing, though. . . ." He hesitated.

"And that is?" Missie prompted.

"Well, I jest told the Lord thet iffen He had a place fer me—wherever it was—I'd be happy to do whatever I could. I don't expect it to be in a church, Missie, but there's lots of folks who need God who never come lookin' fer Him in a church."

"I'm glad, Henry," Missie said softly. "I'm glad you feel that way. And you're right. God needs lots of us—everywhere—to touch other people's hearts."

Missie turned back to finish up the breakfast preparations, and Henry settled himself on a low stool. It wasn't long until Missie heard a cheery whistle and knew Willie would soon join them.

Willie's whistle changed abruptly when he saw Missie, and he paused to look at her carefully. Then he grinned.

"Yer lookin' right smart this mornin', Mrs. LaHaye."

"Oh, Willie, stop teasing. You've been seeing me in plain dresses and walking shoes for so long you've forgotten what I really look like."

"Then I hope ya remind me often. Looks good, don't she, Henry?" Willie said with a wink.

"I already told her so."

"Oh, ho," Willie laughed. "Now thet young Miss Weiss has favored yer presence, ya think ya can pass out compliments to all of the womenfolk, do ya?"

"Nope," said Henry. "Jest the *special* ones."

Willie laughed again. "Well, she's special, all right."

He kissed Missie on the cheek. Missie leaned primly away. "Really, Willie," she reprimanded. "We don't need to put on a show for all to see." She busied herself with serving the break-fast.

After they had eaten, then read a portion of Scripture—which Willie ended as he had throughout the journey with the special passage given to them by Missie's father—they had prayer together.

"Will ya be needin' me today?" Henry asked Willie as Missie began clearing up.

Willie thought a moment. "No, I can manage carin' fer the stock. Go ahead. Make any plans ya want to."

"Thanks. I reckon I'll give the Weisses a hand at gettin' settled in town. They did manage to find a house—such as it is."

"Is Mrs. Emory gonna stay with 'em?"

"No, and she needs some settlin', too. She found a small room over the general store, but there's not much furniture there to speak of. She's already signed up to teach school come fall, but until then she's gonna work in the hotel kitchen."

"The kitchen? Seems rather heavy, burdensome work for such a genteel little woman," Missie commented doubtfully.

"Thet's what I thought. But the job is there—an' she insists."

Missie detected genuine concern in Henry's voice.

He put on his hat. "Well, iffen yer sure I'm not needed, I'll git on over there an' give 'em a hand."

"He's got it right bad, hasn't he?" Willie remarked with an arched brow after Henry had walked away. "Well, Mrs. LaHaye, may I escort ya into town? I take it ya didn't git all prettied up jest to sit out in the sun."

"I think, sir, that I might consent to that," Missie replied playfully.

Missie found the town much as she had expected. There seemed to be very little that was green. A few small gardens looked parched under the sun-drenched sky. The vegetables fighting for an existence were dwarfed and scraggly. Here and there some brave grass put in an appearance—under a dripping pump or close to a watering trough. As far as Missie could see, there had been no attempt to plant trees or shrubbery. Puffs of dust scattered whenever the wind stirred.

The buildings, too, were bleak. No bright paint or fancy signs. Square, bold letters spelled SALOON over a gray, wind-worn building. Another sign announced HOTEL. Missie winced to think of Melinda Emory working in a hot, stuffy kitchen making meals for the guests. Several other weathered buildings lined the dusty streets. There were sidewalks, fairly new, but they, too, were layered with dust except where women's skirts had whisked them clean.

More than one saloon lined the main street. In fact, Missie counted five. *What does such a town need with five saloons?* she wondered. It certainly was not nearly as blessed with churches, but Missie did spy a small spire reaching up from among the buildings huddled over to her left.

There were blacksmith shops—at least three—but maybe, as Mr. Weiss had said, a town this size could use another.

A bank, a sheriff's office, a printshop, a telegraph office, liveries, a stagecoach landing, and an assortment of stores and other buildings that Missie had not yet identified filled out the downtown area. Missie smiled as she read the notice, *Overland Stagecoaches,* and wondered where on earth they took passengers way out in the middle of nowhere.

The fact was, the town didn't interest her much at this point. She still dreaded the fact that she had to stay in it for three months without Willie. She didn't want this town. She wanted Willie's land, the place where she intended to make a home. It would be so different there. The cool valley, the green grass, and Willie's beloved hills, rolling away to the mountains.

Missie could hardly wait for a glimpse of those mountains.

"The Taylorsons live jest down here," Willie announced, interrupting her thoughts. He made a right-hand turn, and soon they were walking down a street lined with houses. There were no sidewalks, but the street was smooth, though as dusty as the rest of the area.

"Thet there is where the doc lives. He has a couple a' rooms for his office in the sheriff's, but he also has one room there at the front of his house fer off-hour treatin'."

Missie let her glance slide over the doctor's residence. The house was unpretentious.

"An' here we are," Willie said cheerfully and opened a gate. Missie stared at the house. It was of unpainted lumber, big and sturdy looking, but as barren as the rest of the town. The two passed by a bit of a garden that seemed to be struggling valiantly for existence. Missie remembered Marty's full, healthy vegetable garden at home.

"My, things are awfully dry!" she ventured.

"They git a little short on water here 'bouts."

Willie rapped on the door and a plump, pleasant-faced woman opened it.

"Oh," she said with a smile, "ya brought yer little wife." Her gaze traveled over Missie. "She is in the family way, all right."

Missie felt the color rush to her face.

"This is Mrs. Taylorson, Missie," Willie said carefully, obviously attempting to ease over the situation. "An' this is my wife—Mrs. LaHaye."

Missie was glad Willie had introduced her as *Mrs. LaHaye*. Somehow it made her feel more grown-up and less like an awkward schoolgirl.

"Come on in," Mrs. Taylorson said, "an' I'll show ya yer room."

She turned and tramped up the stairs to the left of the hall, puffing as she climbed. At the top of the stairs she again took a left turn and pushed open a door. The room was stifling hot, the only window shut tight. It was a plain room, but it was clean. The bed looked old but rather comfortable. Mrs. Taylorson seemed like a no-nonsense person.

"Yer husband said ya had yer own things," said Mrs. Taylorson, "so I jest took out the beddin' an' such."

"Yes, I do," Missie answered, wondering why the faded curtains at the window had escaped Mrs. Taylorson's clean sweep. "It will be just fine."

"I don't usually keep boarders," she said, "but yer husband seemed in a real need like. An' he said thet ya were clean—an' sensible. So I says, 'Okay, I'll give it a try.'" She looked Missie over once more.

"One must have rules, though, when one has boarders," she continued, "so I've made 'em up an' posted 'em here. Don't expect this third one will bother ya much, ya bein' the way ya are, but one never knows—an' one needs rules. I'll leave ya now to look over things an' decide what ya want to be bringin' in. I'll go put on some tea."

She stepped out of the room, and they were alone.

Missie wanted to cry, but she fought against it. She must keep herself well in hand.

Willie went over to the window and threw it wide open. Missie turned to the posted list, headed "Twelve Rules of This House."

"Uh-oh," she said, "you just broke rule number one."

Willie quickly was at her side.

" 'Number one,' " Missie read. " 'Do not leave window open; the dust blows in!' "

" 'Number two: No loud talking or laughing,' " Willie said, picking up with the next one.

"Number three: 'No having men to your room or going out with them, excepting your husband.'" Missie turned to Willie. "I guess you're legal."

They continued down the list, alternating the reading.

"'All water must be used *at least twice* before it is thrown out. We're powerful short, you know.'"

"'Mealtimes are eight, twelve-thirty, and six, and must be strictly kept. It bothers Mr. T's ulcer to be kept waiting.'"

"'Bedtime is ten.'"

"'Borders'—look at the spelling of that. Makes me feel like a bunch of petunias," Missie commented. " 'Borders are expected to attend church on Sundays.'"

"'Rent must be paid in advance.'" Then Willie added, "I'll take care of it."

"'No borrowing money or property.'"

" 'Border must care for her own personal needs and clothes.'"

"'Hair can be washed at back-door basin—once a week.'"

"'Number twelve'—I guess she ran out of ideas," Missie said. "There's nothing listed here for number twelve."

"Good," Willie said. "Then I won't be breakin' a rule when I kiss ya." He pulled Missie into his arms.

Missie struggled against her tears as Willie held her close. She was glad he did not release her right away. It gave her time to regain her composure. At last she stepped back and smiled.

"I'll bet if she'd thought of it, that would have been on the list," she said. Willie grinned and kissed her again.

Willie and Missie went downstairs and promptly settled the account. Missie could have cried as she watched him pay for three long months. How could she ever bear it? She would die of loneliness. She turned her back and bit her lips in an effort to keep herself under control.

Mrs. Taylorson tucked the money into the bosom of her

dress and smiled warmly at the couple.

Mrs. Taylorson insisted that Missie move in right away. The day would be spent in sorting out what Missie would need and getting her settled. There was no rule about sewing machines, but just to be safe, Missie asked. She was pleased Mrs. Taylorson did not object to having hers in the room. Missie would appreciate her machine, which would help fill the hours while she sewed for her coming baby.

Mrs. Taylorson informed them they would be expected for the evening meal at six o'clock sharp. She would see them then. If they needed assistance in the meantime, they could feel free to knock on the kitchen door.

Willie drove their wagon back up the street in front of the Taylorsons' home, and the sorting began. It was hard to decide what should go and what should stay. Missie tended to want to send everything, and Willie kept thinking of things she might need or long for. At last they reached a compromise, and Missie was soon settled into the small upstairs room. Willie, too, moved in his few needs for the one week he would share the room with Missie. He then returned the wagon to the outskirts of the town, where it was left in Henry's care.

Promptly at six the LaHayes descended the steps toward the hall. Finding the dining room was not difficult with the aroma of home-cooked food guiding them. They entered the room and found the table set for four.

A gentleman was already seated, fork in hand, but he did have the courtesy to lay down his fork and rise to his feet as the couple entered. It wasn't exactly a smile that crossed his face to welcome them, but neither was it a frown.

"Howdya do," he said officiously, extending a hand to Willie. "I'm J. B. Taylorson."

Missie wondered what the *J. B.* was for.

"I'm William LaHaye—an' this is my wife, Melissa," Willie

responded. Missie didn't dare look at "William," or she would have started giggling.

Mr. Taylorson nodded to the chairs, "Won't ya sit down." It was plain he wanted to get on with the business of eating.

Willie seated Missie and took the chair beside her just as Mrs. Taylorson entered from the kitchen with a bowl of food in each hand.

"Here ya are," she said. "I told Ben thet I told ya six sharp."

So the *B* was for Ben. That still left the *J*.

Mrs. Taylorson settled herself, and Mr. Taylorson blessed the food in a rather perfunctory manner—the same way he said his "howdy." Once the formality was over, his full attention was given to the meal. The beans, potatoes, and meat were simply prepared, yet tasty, and very welcome after the monotonous trail fare.

Mrs. Taylorson allowed no slack in the conversation. Her questions followed so closely on the heels of the previous one that there was scarcely time for a civil reply. She offered many suggestions as to what a mother-to-be should be eating and doing, and most of them made a lot of sense.

After the meal was over, Mr. Taylorson slid back his chair and pulled a pipe from his pocket.

"Now, Ben," Mrs. Taylorson chided, "smoke's not good fer a woman in Mrs. LaHaye's condition. Why don't ya take thet on out to the porch?"

Missie felt embarrassed. "That's fine, Mrs. Taylorson. We don't want to drive your husband from his own home. Willie and I were thinking of a walk, anyway."

But Mr. Taylorson had already risen. "I'd rather smoke on the porch enyhow—git out of this insufferable heat." He gathered his pipe and tobacco and headed for the door. "You smoke?" he asked Willie.

"No, sir."

"Ya can join me enyway iffen you'd like."

Willie followed him out, and Missie began to help Mrs. Taylorson clear the table.

"Now, now," Mrs. Taylorson said in alarm. "Yer room-and-board payment doesn't say enything 'bout deductions fer yer help."

Missie stammered, "I . . . I wasn't thinking of deductions. I just thought I could give you a hand."

"Fine, fine, iffen ya wish to, but it ain't called fer—an' it won't change a thing."

Missie helped carry the leftover food and the dishes to the kitchen. It really was unbearably hot. She finally excused herself and went to find Willie. She really did want a walk.

The first thing Willie said when they were alone was that he felt greatly relieved to know Missie would be well cared for. She wanted to answer that she would just as soon take care of herself, thank you just the same. But she held her tongue. She knew this arrangement and separation was very hard for Willie, too, and he was doing it only because of necessity. Doing it for her. Missie decided she would work at making these last days together peaceful and cheerful.

THIRTEEN

News

Amid the busyness of getting ready to leave with the south-bound supply train at the end of the week, Willie burst through the bedroom door. Missie looked up at him from her sewing machine.

"Guess what?" he exclaimed.

"Whatever it is, it must really be something," Missie answered with puzzled surprise.

"It is! It really is! I went in to thet telegraph place uptown and I found out thet fer only a few cents we can send a telegram back home."

"Back home?"

"Yep! Right to yer folks. The office in town there will git the message to 'em. So I figured as how we should do jest thet."

"What would we say?"

"Jest let 'em know thet we made it safe an' sound . . . an' . . . maybe tell 'em about the baby."

"Oh, Willie," Missie cried, "could we?"

"Grab whatever ya need an' let's go."

Missie quickly smoothed her hair, then picked up a light cotton bonnet. Just in time she remembered the window and gently closed it just in case Mrs. Taylorson should check her room while she was gone.

"Slow down some," Willie cautioned with a chuckle. "It

ain't gonna go away." Then he continued, "The man says thet ya have ten words."

"Oh, dear," Missie sighed, "how are we going to say everything we want to tell them in ten words?"

They reached the office, and Willie opened the door for Missie. She couldn't have said if her breathlessness was due to their brisk walk or her excitement.

They labored together over the wording, composing and changing, recomposing and changing again. Finally they felt they had done the best they could. Willie handed the message and the money to the man behind the desk.

"ISAIAH 41:10," the message read. "MISSIE REMAINS TETTSFORD STOP GRANDCHILD DUE OCTOBER STOP INFORM PA."

Missie felt her heart constrict with emotion as she envisioned her parents' excitement and relief at receiving the telegram, then passing the news on to Willie's pa.

"Oh, Willie," Missie asked, "do you think Pa LaHaye will mind getting the message secondhand?"

"Iffen I know my pa," Willie said, "he'd think me a squanderin' ignoramus iffen I sent two of 'em to the same town."

"When will it get there?"

"Fella says if no lines are down and there's no other trouble, they should have it in a couple a' days." He took her arm and turned her toward the door of the telegraph office. "Now I'll walk ya on back to the Taylorsons' and then git back to the figurin' an' loadin' of my supplies."

"No need to go with me. I'll find my way back and just take my time. Where's Henry?"

"He's over at the smithy's. He's been a powerful help to me. I don't know what I'da done without 'im."

"Has he been callin' again?"

"Iffen ya mean has he been to town, yes. I haven't asked him his doin's."

Missie smiled. "It's not really that hard to figure out, is it?"

"Poor Henry," said Willie, "he has my sympathy. Once one of you pretty little things gits yer fingers all twisted up in a fella's heart, he's a goner. Well, I'll see ya at six."

Missie turned to walk back to the Taylorsons' lighthearted in spite of the oppressive heat at this small but satisfying link to the family back home.

She tried again to picture her pa and ma when they received the telegram. It wasn't hard to imagine it. They'd stop whatever they were doing and thank God for His care for their children, and they would pray for the new baby. Missie felt both joy and sadness together.

When she reached her room she was no longer in the mood for sewing. She opened her window wide and lay down on the bed.

In a very few days the supply train would be going south, with Willie following. How she wished she could go, as well. The absurd notion of trying to stow away crossed her mind. Once he discovered her, Willie would simply turn around and bring her back. No, there seemed no way out. Willie would go, and she would have to stay.

"God," she prayed, "that help you're promising . . . I'm really needing it right now." The tears were again pushing behind her eyelids when Missie heard heavy steps on the stairs. She quickly went to the window and closed it.

"Ya got visitors," Mrs. Taylorson called. "Seein' as how they're ladies, I gave 'em the privilege of the parlor."

Missie hurried down. To her joy she found Kathy Weiss and Melinda Emory.

She greeted them eagerly, exchanging a quick hug with each young woman in turn.

"Henry told us where to find ya," Kathy explained.

"Oh, I'm so glad you came," Missie said. "I was up in my room lying down, and I confess I was beginning to feel sorry for myself."

Melinda Emory took her hand with great empathy. "And you have reason to. If I were you, I'd be feeling the same way."

"Would you?" Missie swallowed a lump in her throat as she looked into the face of the newly widowed woman. Her separation from Willie, difficult though it was, had a reunion time at the end of it.

Melinda was nodding her head in answer to Missie's question, and tears gathered in her eyes. "I would. In fact, I'm not sure I would stand for it at all."

"Oh, I tried to argue, but Willie just wouldn't hear of it," Missie said, shaking her head. "He's downright unreasonable about things . . . well, since Becky . . ."

"I can understand how Willie feels," Kathy said. "An' as hard as it is, I think he might be right."

"Of course he is," Melinda said. "Men *usually* are in this kind of situation. It's just very difficult for us women, that's all. We're too sentimental to be practical."

Missie nodded. "I guess that's so," she said, "and I'm afraid I have made it rather hard for Willie."

"I don't suppose he expected you to stay without *some* resistance," Kathy comforted.

Melinda then asked, "Are you all settled?"

"Yes . . . I guess so," Missie responded, glad for the change of subject. "I kept as few things as I could so it wouldn't mean too much trouble later. I did keep my sewing machine. Willie thought it would help me to be busy—and I do need to do the sewing for the baby. Anyway, I love to sew."

"So do I," Melinda said with fervor. "I had a machine. . . ." Her voice drifted to a halt, and there was an awkward pause among the three at another reminder of Melinda's tragic loss.

Missie then spoke up. "Oh, if you'd like to use my machine—anytime. I would be so pleased to have your company."

"Could I?"

"Please do! The little bit of sewing I have to do will never keep me busy for the whole three months."

Melinda smiled. "Thank you so much, Mrs. LaHaye. I would so appreciate that."

"Please, call me Missie."

"And my name is Melinda. You can even shorten it if you like."

"Melinda suits you. I like it."

Melinda smiled.

"I heard you found employment," Missie continued.

"Yes, of a sort."

"It must be awfully tiring."

"It is that, but at least I'm paying my own way, and it won't be long until school starts. With my salary from the hotel—an' your sewing machine—perhaps I can start school in style." She gave a small chuckle.

"I was a schoolteacher, too—before I married Willie."

"Really? And a good one, I'm sure."

"I hope so. At any rate, I loved it. Some days I miss it."

"I wish I had some trainin' like thet," Kathy remarked. "I'd love to git a position to help Pa out fer a while. But the only work thet is available fer a girl here, iffen she doesn't have special trainin' . . . well, Pa won't hear tell of it."

"Your pa will make out just fine, I'm sure," Melinda comforted. "In no time at all he'll have all the business he can handle."

Kathy smiled hopefully. "Yeah, I reckon he will. Still, I'd like to do more than just keep house."

"Do you like to sew?" asked Missie.

"I've never learned, so I really don't know."

"Well, why don't I teach you? Between Melinda and you and me, we'll really keep my machine humming."

They all laughed.

"Could ya? I mean, would ya mind?"

"Of course not. I'd love to."

"Then I'd love it, too."

Mrs. Taylorson bustled through the door.

"I brung you girls some tea," she said, carrying a tray of cups. "Company don't come to my house an' not git served— even iffen it ain't my company."

"Oh, Mrs. Taylorson, how kind!" Missie exclaimed, pleased that her landlady was so thoughtful. She introduced her friends and explained to Mrs. Taylorson that she might see them often. Mrs. Taylorson seemed to enjoy the idea. It occurred to Missie that the woman might not have much company of her own and was welcoming the idea of some female companionship.

The women continued their visit over their tea and cookies, including Mrs. Taylorson in their conversation.

At length the two visitors rose to leave. They requested that Missie visit them, which she promised to do.

Mrs. Taylorson eagerly invited them to return "jest anytime."

Missie climbed the stairs to her room feeling much better. It had been a good day. God had given the help He'd promised. The telegram home, the visit with friends—a reminder that she would not really be alone when Willie left—these were gentle kindnesses given from the hand of a loving Father. With all these blessings, Missie felt a warm glow inside.

But as she closed the door to her room, the thought of Willie's impending departure hit her once more. How was she ever going to manage three long months without him?

She moved over to the window and stared out over the rather bleak scene below her, trying to recapture the truth of her heavenly Father's care and presence. She turned at a noise from the stairway to find Willie entering the room to deposit a strange heap on the floor.

"What's that?" she asked, pointing at what looked like a bundle of canvas.

"The gear I'll be needin'."

"Gear?"

"Fer ridin', once I'm at the ranch."

"You're going to ride in *that*?"

"Sure am. It might look a bit strange, but it's a cowboy's best friend out on the range."

"What is it?" Missie asked skeptically. "And how do you use it?"

Willie lifted the canvas. "It's chaps," he explained. "Ya jest pull 'em on over yer trousers, like so. The heavy canvas sheds the rain, takes the spines of the cactus, and keeps all manner of weather and injury from a rider. Ya really ought to have some yerself."

Missie laughed and then pointed to a square of red material. "And what's that?" she asked again.

"A bandanna. Ya wear it round yer neck—tied loosely like this." Willie demonstrated. "When ya get drivin' them little doggies an' the dust flies so ya can hardly breathe, ya just pull it up over yer mouth an' nose—like this!"

Missie giggled. "I thought that's what you use when you're holding up a bank."

"Guess a few have used it fer thet, as well." Willie smiled with her. "I'll remember thet, should I ever think of holdin' up a bank."

Missie laughed again and then turned for a good look at the strange apparel. It was going to take some getting used to—

seeing Willie decked out in these strange canvas pants. She tried to imagine herself in them and smiled softly.

"Reckon for now," she said, "I'll just plan to fight the cactus and the rain without the help of those."

FOURTEEN

Sunday

On Sunday morning Willie and Missie prepared themselves and headed for the church spire they had seen. The building looked bare and drab on the outside, but inside the clean-swept wooden floor and carefully dusted benches showed that someone did indeed care for this simple house of worship in this frontier town. Henry, Mr. Weiss and Kathy, Melinda Emory, and the LaHayes added considerably to the small congregation, and they were welcomed from the platform at the beginning of the service.

The pastor, getting on in years, seemed rather weary, Missie thought. But when he rose to preach, fire was in his voice, and his face came alive with passion for the truth he was presenting. Missie was overjoyed to be in a real church service and hear a true sermon once again. She had appreciated the Sunday services of the wagon train, but she had missed having a pastor speak from the Word of God.

The reverend greeted each one kindly at the door and personally invited the newcomers to return. Willie explained that he would not be around for another Sunday, but he was sure Missie would be there faithfully.

"We shall welcome you," the old gentleman said with warmth. "And if you should ever need a friend, my wife and I would be happy to have you to our home, as well."

Missie thanked him for his generosity and stepped out into the shining day.

"Anything you'd be carin' to do today?" Willie asked as they walked through the dust and heat back to the Taylorsons' and their rented room.

"Oh yes," said Missie with a sigh, "I'd like to go for a long walk among some cool trees, or picnic beside a stream, or maybe just lie beside a spring and watch the water gurgle."

"Missie"—Willie shook his head—"don't, *please* don't say things like that. . . ."

"I'm sorry," Missie whispered quickly. She tried hard to think of something that could actually be done and enjoyed in the heat of this drab town.

"We could call on the Weisses," she finally suggested.

"All right," Willie agreed enthusiastically, no doubt relieved she had thought of something. "I sure do hope Henry won't think I'm spyin' on 'im." He caught her hand in his with a chuckle.

That afternoon at the Weisses, they received such a hearty welcome Missie's spirits lifted even without green grass or a stream. Henry was there, also, though he didn't seem one bit put out to have his boss appear. Melinda Emory was there, too, so the six of them settled in for a good visit. Kathy served them all cold tea, declaring the day far too warm for hot tea or coffee.

Missie was surprised at the time when Kathy asked if they could all stay for supper.

"Oh, I don't think we can," Missie said. "We didn't say anything to Mrs. Taylorson, and supper is served at six."

She and Willie exchanged smiles.

"How 'bout I run over an' inform yer good landlady?" Henry asked.

"Oh, but—"

"Please stay," Kathy begged. "The men will be gone by next Sunday."

"Well, I'm not sure what she'll think," Missie said uncertainly, "but . . . well . . . all right. She probably hasn't started to actually prepare it, so she shouldn't mind, should she?"

It turned out that both Henry and Willie walked back together while the girls went to the kitchen to give Kathy a hand.

Mrs. Taylorson did not object. In fact, Willie got the impression she was relieved at not having to fuss about in a hot kitchen on such a warm evening.

Kathy's meal of fried chicken, hot biscuits, and gravy was served with love and laughter, and everyone enjoyed the time spent together.

"I know," Kathy suggested after the dishes had been washed, "let's have a time of singing, for old times' sake."

The rest agreed. Henry went for his guitar while Mr. Weiss tuned up his violin.

They sang all the songs they had enjoyed together from their trip west—folk songs, love songs, dance tunes, and hymns. When they were finished, they sang their favorite ones all over again.

It was late when Willie and Missie walked back to the Taylorsons' hand in hand.

"I'm afraid we've broken rule number six," Missie said.

"An' what is thet?"

"Bedtime is at ten o'clock," Missie replied in a mock stern voice. She broke into giggles, then quickly checked herself and added, "We'd better be careful or we'll break number two, as well."

"An' thet is . . ."

"No loud talking or laughing," Missie said, effecting a gruff, deep voice again.

"Ya little goose," Willie said, putting his arm around her waist and drawing her close. "Do ya have 'em all memorized by number?"

"I think so. I've read them often enough."

"Speakin' of readin'," Willie said, "ya really should have somethin' on hand to read. I'll talk to the preacher. He may have a good idea of what books can be had. He may even have some—"

"Oh, Willie, stop fretting about me. I've got all that sewing to do, and all that yarn to be knitted up, a piano to learn to play, and sewing lessons to give. Surely it will keep me busy."

"Well, we want to be sure," said Willie, giving her hand a little squeeze.

When Willie returned to their room on Wednesday evening, he quietly told Missie that the supply train was all loaded up and would be pulling out early the next morning. Missie knew he was keeping his voice even and matter-of-fact for her sake, but she had to bite her lip all evening to keep the tears from overflowing during supper with the Taylorsons. She hoped Willie didn't notice, but of course he did. They retired to their room soon after the meal was finished so Willie could get his belongings packed up. It didn't take long. Time suddenly seemed to be heavy on their hands.

"It's strange," Missie said as she stood and gazed out the window, "our time is so short and precious, and yet one doesn't really know how to spend it."

"Have ya everything ya need?" asked Willie for the umpteenth time, coming over to stand beside her.

"I'm sure I will be fine."

"Well, I'll leave ya some money, jest in case."

"Really, Willie, I don't think I'll be needing—"

"Ya never know. Maybe somethin' will turn up thet ya be needin' or wantin'—an' you'll need some fer the church offerin'."

Missie only nodded.

Willie led her over to the one chair in the room and sat near her on the bed. "I'm sure glad thet Kathy an' Melinda will be around."

"Me too."

"I hope ya see 'em real often."

"Melinda will be working—but she promised to come over of an evening to sew."

"An' Kathy is free to come anytime—right?"

Missie nodded again. "The first thing she wants to sew is curtains for her kitchen window."

"An' ya can visit 'em at their places, too," continued Willie.

Missie agreed.

"Ya might pay a call on the preacher an' his wife, too. They seem like real nice folks. Jest don't stay out after dark—please, Missie?"

"I won't. Promise."

"One can't be too careful."

"*You're* the one that needs to be careful, Willie! Here I am, all tucked away safe in a town, where the worst that can happen to me is to get dust in my eyes—and you're telling *me* to be careful. It's you that's going to have to take care, Willie." Missie swallowed hard over the lump in her throat as Willie smoothed her hair.

"Won't much happen to me," he assured her. "I'm travelin' south with a whole passel of supply wagons, an' Henry'll be with me once we reach our spread. No need to worry none 'bout me."

"I s'pose so," Missie admitted. "I just won't be able to keep from it, though."

"I'll worry, too," Willie said, his voice husky. "It doesn't pleasure me none to leave ya, Missie. If only there was some other way—"

"I'll be fine," Missie quickly assured him, trying for his sake to say the words as though she really meant them.

"Missie . . ." Willie hesitated, reaching over to hold her close. "Missie, the wagons are to pull out real early in the mornin'. I don't intend to wake ya up when I leave, so my good-bye will be tonight. I love ya. I've loved ya ever since ya were a little schoolgirl."

"And you showed it," she whispered, smiling around her tears, "by dunking my hair ribbons in an inkwell."

"An' carvin' our initials—"

"And putting a grasshopper in my lunch pail."

"An' tellin' young Todd Culver thet I'd knock out his teeth iffen he didn't leave my girl alone. An' closin' yer classroom window when it got stuck. An' prayin' fer ya every single day—thet iffen God willed, ya'd learn to love me."

"You did that?" Missie leaned away to look into his face.

"I did."

"Oh, Willie," Missie cried, pressing her face against his shoulder. "I'll miss you so. I can't tell you how much."

When Missie sat up in bed the next morning, she was alone, and Willie's things were gone from the room. An emptiness filled her that she could not have put into words. She turned back into her pillow and sobbed. How would she ever cope? She missed him so dreadfully already. She had secretly promised herself the night before that she would be sure to waken so she might feel the comfort of Willie's arms once more. She was annoyed at herself for failing to rouse, yet finally she had to admit it would not have made it any easier to say good-bye again.

If only I was at home with Mama and Pa to console me. . . .

They would understand about pain and separation.

Her parents had personally known grief—far more devastating and final than her own sorrow now. They had lived through it. And she could, too. After all, Willie *would* be coming back. The wait wouldn't be so long—not really.

She forced herself to crawl out of bed, then bathed her face at the basin. She caught herself wondering if this was wash number one or two for this water, and if she could now throw it out and get some fresh. Her eyes moved to Mrs. Taylorson's list. The empty space for number twelve now had some writing beside it. Had Mrs. Taylorson come up with another rule? Missie crossed the room for a better look and read number twelve aloud: "Always remember that I love you—both of you."

"Oh, Willie, ya silly goose!" she cried as fresh tears streamed down her newly washed cheeks. She was going to have to wash her face again before going down for breakfast. That, for sure, would entitle her to some more water.

FIFTEEN

Surprises

Missie put her mind to settling in alone for the long stay. First she decided to list all the "must-do's" on a piece of paper. Then she listed all the "want-to-do's." Neither list seemed very long. How would those tasks and activities ever keep her occupied until she was free to leave this town? She laid the lists aside with a sigh and went to her sewing material.

She spread out all the fabric she had purchased and mentally planned just what she would sew from each piece. She then checked her yarn and noted the articles she would knit or crochet. She took a fresh sheet of paper for her weekly visitation list—one call per week on Kathy and Melinda and at least one call *from* them in return to use Missie's machine.

She sketched out a complete week on a piece of paper with a space for each hour of the day, and then she filled in her proposed activities: sewing, sewing lessons, knitting, laundry, reading, visits, shopping (she didn't know what for, but it filled a space and the walk would do her good). She even included time at the piano in her hopes for learning to play a bit. Her week still had many vacant hours, and she didn't see how she could stretch out her plans to fill them.

She juggled, rearranged, and stretched all she could and finally filled in all the extra spots with the words "free time" and tried to convince herself that somehow "free time" should be looked forward to as a special liberty. Maybe Willie was right after all about checking with the pastor and his wife for some reading materials.

She had scheduled sewing for her first morning, so she began on a small blanket. As simple as the project was, she just couldn't keep her mind on it, so she laid it aside. She picked up her Bible once more and opened the pages at random. She tried to concentrate on the words, but the words blurred in her mind.

"It's just no use," she muttered, grabbing up some knitting. "I just can't think clearly!"

She had added only a few stitches to the sock she was making when Mrs. Taylorson called up the stairs, "Ya have a caller, miss."

Missie so wished Mrs. Taylorson wouldn't call her "miss," as though she were still a young girl instead of a grown married woman. She smoothed her hair back and made her way down the steps.

Kathy Weiss was waiting for her in the parlor. Missie almost cried with relief at seeing her friend so soon after the men had left.

"Did you come to sew the curtains?" she asked after greeting Kathy.

"Goodness, no! I don't think I could concentrate on sewin' anything today. I jest had to go out fer a while, an' I thought maybe you'd be needin' it, as well."

"You're absolutely right," Missie said emphatically. "Just let me get my bonnet."

The two young women strolled through the streets of the dusty town, chatting as they browsed along the storefronts. Occasionally they wandered inside to peruse the merchandise. Neither of them purchased a thing, but Missie returned home in better spirits, and Kathy promised to return that very evening for her first sewing lesson.

That afternoon Missie sat down and made herself a calendar, one page for each of the three months ahead of her. She marked each day's date in big numbers, wrote Willie's name beside the first one—August second—then circled October twenty-fifth. It was as close as she could figure the baby's arrival date to be. In between the two dates stretched many weeks and days and hours. But Missie intended to strike them off, one by one, in hopes they would move quickly to the next one.

It was awfully warm in the room, and Missie was feeling emotionally and physically exhausted, so she took off her shoes and stretched out on the bed to rest.

"It all will be worth it," she told herself aloud. "By the time Willie comes for me and the baby, he'll have our house ready. I'll be able to move right in, instead of living cramped in that old wagon. Just think—our own home! I'll hang up the curtains Mama helped me sew, spread out the cozy rugs, make up the bed with all those warm quilts. I'll put my dishes in the cupboards, set up the sewing machine, put all the crocks and barrels in my pantry—all those things I'll be needing in my very own home."

She let the happy thoughts drive away the loneliness and drifted off to sleep.

Kathy came that evening as promised. Having never used a sewing machine before, she had a bit of difficulty in catching on to the rhythm of the foot treadle, but eventually she had a good start on her curtains.

Day one was finally over. With relief Missie crossed it off her new calendar and knelt beside her bed. Somewhere out there, in the dark, distant night, she knew Willie would be remembering her in prayer, as well. It helped to ease her loneliness.

At the end of each slow-moving day, Missie struck the numbers from the calendar in the manner of a general triumphant after battle. She had survived her first Sunday alone, her first hair washing, and her first washday. She was working on her third day at the piano when Mrs. Taylorson called, "Miss, ya have a feller here with a telygram."

Missie fairly flew to the door. What news could be so important that it needed to reach her by telegram? Her heart thumped wildly within her, every beat crying, "Willie! Willie!" She quickly took the telegram with a shaking hand and scanned the small sheet.

"RECEIVED MESSAGE STOP PRAISE GOD STOP HAPPY AND CONCERNED ABOUT BABY STOP ISAIAH," she read.

"Mama and Pa!" she exclaimed. To the waiting Mrs. Taylorson, she said, "It's from my folks—they've just acknowledged our message." The woman smiled and nodded in an understanding way, and Missie smiled back and hurried up the stairs to her room. Once inside, with the door closed behind her, she crushed the blessed message to her breast and fell to her knees beside her bed, tears falling unchecked.

"Oh, Mama . . . Pa . . . I miss you both so much, and I love you so. Oh . . . if only . . ."

Missie posted the telegram beneath Willie's rule number twelve. Many times a day she would read it and think of the dear ones who had sent it to her.

As the days were gradually crossed off on Missie's calendar, her pile of sewn articles and knitted things increased. Kathy had come often, and soon she had progressed to sewing dresses when the curtains and some aprons were finished.

Melinda also had spent evenings with Missie. Her job in the hotel kitchen had taxed her limited strength, so she never dared to stay very late. But eventually she had managed with her small income to buy yard goods for three attractive dresses and sew them up for use in the schoolroom. When September came, her days as restaurant cook and dishwasher were over at last, and she was happily employed as the town's new schoolmarm.

Missie twice had called on the preacher and his wife. She not only found their company delightfully refreshing, but they loaned her several books from their own library. They also returned each call, and Mrs. Taylorson was quite beside herself to have a real parson in her parlor.

After Missie had put on her nightgown and brushed her hair before bed one night, she stood studying her calendar. It was now September eighth.

"September eighth is a long way from August second," she whispered to herself. "Not halfway yet, but almost . . . almost." She made a long black mark through the number and went to kneel beside her bed. As she was praying, she heard a gentle rap on her door. Missie looked up in surprise. She hadn't heard any footsteps on the stairs.

Then the door opened, and there stood Willie. Paralyzed with shock, Missie remained on her knees and just stared.

Not one to wait for her bidding, he quickly was at her side and whisked her to her feet.

"It's really you!" Missie gasped. "It's really you!" And then she was in his arms, clinging to him, sobbing into his jacket while he showered kisses on her face, stroked her hair, and rocked her gently back and forth.

"I jest couldn't stand it anymore," he said huskily.

"You came for me?"

"Oh no," Willie corrected hurriedly. "Just to *see* you, thet's all. I was jest so lonesome thet Henry finally said, 'Why don't ya make yerself a little trip? Ya ain't rightly of much use here anyway.' So I did."

"Where's Henry?"

"I left him workin' on the corrals."

Missie laughed. "Don't know how you ever got away without Henry. Why, he must be near as lonesome as you."

"He did send a couple of letters with me—*three,* in fact. He sent you one, too."

Missie laughed again. "Dear old Henry—and he sent *two* others?"

"Yep. One to the Weisses and one to Melinda."

"He's just writing to *all* his friends."

"But I want to hear 'bout *you,*" Willie said firmly, swinging her around. "How ya been?"

"Lonesome!" Missie said fervently.

"Me too," Willie replied. "Me too." And he kissed her again.

"How long can you stay?"

"Just till day after tomorrow."

"Only one day?" Missie's lips started to tremble.

Willie nodded. "I gotta git back, Missie. I shouldn'ta come, really. We've got so much to do 'fore winter sets in, but . . . well, I jest couldn't stay away. I've *gotta* leave mornin' after next."

"Do you have a place to live out there?"

"A temporary one—that's the way most folks do. Then they build later—as they can."

"And the cattle?"

"Only a few head. We can't really take on too many until we're ready for 'em, an' then ya need men to care for 'em, too. After that ya need a bunkhouse to bed the men."

"How many men?"

"Four or five at first."

"Ya mean I'm going to be cooking for six or seven men?" Missie's shock caused her to step back.

"No, silly," Willie said as he pulled her back against him. "The cook does thet in the cook shack."

"You must have a cook shack, too?"

"Yeah, an' we hafta git all thet ready this fall."

Missie took his hand, and they sat down on the edge of the bed.

"Didn't realize it took that many men to run a ranch," she said thoughtfully.

"Should rightly have more than thet, but I'm gonna try to make do fer the time bein'."

"What on earth do they all do?"

"Need shifts, fer one thing. Always should be some of 'em out there ridin' herd on things—watchin' the cattle an' keepin' an eye out fer trouble."

"Trouble—you mean like wild animals and things?"

"I s'pose wild animals enter into it, but they're not the greatest danger."

"What then?"

Willie grinned. "Accordin' to what I hear, a rancher's biggest threat comes from *tame* animals."

"What do you mean?"

"Rustlers."

"Rustlers?"

"Yep. More than one rancher has been driven from the land—forced to give up an' move on out—because of rustlers."

"That's horrible!" Missie exclaimed. "Do they carry guns?"

"Reckon they do," Willie said calmly.

"But what do we do?" Missie could not let the matter drop. "Will you order your men to carry guns?"

"My men won't need those orders. They'll be used to havin' a gun hangin' from their saddle."

"But . . . but, would they *kill* someone?" Missie could hardly force the word out.

"My men will have orders never to shoot to kill another human bein'," Willie said firmly, "even iffen it means losin' the whole herd."

"Might they do that—the rustlers, I mean? Might they take the whole herd?"

"Not usually. They normally just drive off a few at a time. Pickin' on stragglers, gradually workin' at a herd—especially one that isn't carefully watched. Sometimes their need—or their greed—drives 'em to make a bold move and try fer the entire lot."

"Oh, Willie, what will we do if—"

"Now, let's not borrow trouble," Willie said soothingly. "We'll hire the men we can and protect the herd the best we can. Thet's all we can do."

"But how can you afford to pay all those men?"

" 'Fraid a cowboy don't make all thet much. Works out nice fer the ranchers, but not so great fer the cowboys. They do git their bed and board and enough money to buy the tobacco and few supplies they be needin'. Some even manage to lay a little aside. As to the payin' of 'em, I figured thet cost into my accounts when I was workin' out what we'd be needin'. When we start sellin' cattle of our own, their wages will come from the sales."

Missie was relieved to know Willie had things well under control.

"What else do they do?" she asked, getting back to the cowboys.

"Break horses, build and fix fences, watch fer sickness an' snakes an' varmints. They care for the critters during bad storms an' keep an eye on the pasture and water holes to make sure the cows are well cared for. Their main job, though, is to keep the cows grazin' well together so thet there ain't a lot of stragglers scattered through the hills—easy victims of prowlin' animals an' them rustlers."

"Sounds like a big job to me."

"Yup, it's a big job. But most cowboys wouldn't trade it fer any other job in the world."

"Let's forget cowboys, cook shacks, and bunkhouses," Missie interrupted. "Let's think 'bout us for a while."

Willie agreed as his arm tightened around her. "Yer lookin' good. Feelin' okay?"

"Oh, Willie!" Missie suddenly burst out. "I forgot to show you. Look!" She jumped up and pointed to the telegram on her wall. "Mama and Pa got our message," she reported enthusiastically, "and they sent one of their own!"

Willie grinned as he stood to read the telegram. "Makes 'em seem a lot closer like, don't it?"

Missie nodded.

"This trip made you seem closer, too," said Willie. "Took six days to make it down there by wagon—but I made it back in 'bout half the time on horseback."

"You did? Then it's really not so *awfully* far, is it?" Missie was comforted.

———

Willie climbed on his horse as the sun edged over the horizon. He had spent two nights and a day with Missie. She had wondered if she could face the dreadful agonies of parting again—but it was not as difficult as she had feared. She struck two more days from her calendar as she went to bed that night. She had completely forgotten it during Willie's visit.

———

Missie felt awfully restless. The book she was attempting to read now lay discarded on her pillow. Her sewing projects had all been completed days ago. She wasn't about to buy more fabric for things she really could do without. She had run out of yarn but had no wish to make a trip to the store for more—though that was one item she was certain she could put to good use. Willie always needed a new pair of socks. But, no, she'd wait till she had another reason to shop. Maybe a visit to Kathy's . . . no, her heart just wasn't in it.

Listless, edgy, and out of sorts, she paced her room—back and forth. Maybe she was just tired. When it was twelve-thirty, *sharp*—and time for the noon meal—she knew she wasn't hungry. She called downstairs to Mrs. Taylorson that she didn't feel like eating—could she please be excused? She'd just lie down awhile.

She hadn't been on her bed for long when a sudden contraction tightened her abdomen. To her relief, it soon subsided. Missie closed her eyes and tried to sleep, but before she could drop off, another one shuddered through her.

When this passed, Missie sat up and squinted at her homemade calendar on the wall. "It can't be," she exclaimed aloud, her emotions swinging between delight and dismay. "This is only October tenth. You can't come yet, baby. It just isn't time! It *can't* be!" But Missie soon realized that it was indeed time.

She climbed out of bed and paced for a while, then lay down, only to get up and pace some more.

What will Willie think? she asked herself. *I told him October twenty-fifth—and he said he'd be here on the twenty-second, just to be sure. Maybe I'm just imagining things, or maybe it's a false alarm.*

But it was not a false alarm. Missie's landlady came up the stairs to check on her, and Mrs. Taylorson soon recognized it for what it really was, even though she had never had children of her own. She suggested sending immediately for the doctor, but Missie insisted on waiting. She wanted to be absolutely sure the baby was indeed on its way. At last Mrs. Taylorson could stand the wait no more. She sent poor Mr. Taylorson over for the doctor before the good man could even enjoy his after-supper pipe. To Missie's relief, the doctor was not off tending a gunshot wound or setting a broken bone as she had earlier predicted to Willie, and the doctor came almost at once.

That night, about ten o'clock, a son was born to Missie— two weeks early by her calculations. He was not very big, but he was healthy and strong. His young mother, who had been repeating over and over throughout the delivery, "Fear thou not; for I am with thee," cried tears of joy at her first sight of him.

After the doctor had gone and Missie and the baby were bedded for the night, Mrs. Taylorson still scurried about the room, clucking and fussing like a mother hen.

"He's a dandy little wee'un, ain't he? Whatcha gonna call 'im?"

"I don't know," Missie replied sleepily. "I tried to talk about names with Willie—but he said he'd be here when the baby arrived and we'd pick a name then. After we'd seen the baby."

"But he ain't comin' fer two weeks yet," said the practical Mrs. Taylorson. "Don't seem fittin' thet a child should go fer two whole weeks without a name."

"I know," Missie said, smiling at her son, who lay snuggled up against her. "I guess I'll have to name him."

"Ya got a name picked?"

"One I like. I just *happened* to marry a man with the same middle name as my pa. Now, doesn't it seem fitting that our son should bear that name?"

"'Deed it do!" Mrs. Taylorson exclaimed, clapping her hands. "Yer Willie could hardly fault ya on thet choice. What's the name?"

"Nathan," said Missie. "Nathan." She said it again, savoring the sound of it.

"Nathan?" Mrs. Taylorson repeated and nodded thoughtfully. "Rather nice. I like it. I think it even suits the wee package. Nathan . . . jest Nathan?"

"No, Nathan *Isaiah*."

"Isaiah?" Mrs. Taylorson looked a bit doubtful on this one, but she made no further comment except to ask, "Is Isaiah somethin' special, too?"

"It certainly is," Missie said with a catch in her voice. "Very special."

Missie pulled the covers about herself and her small son. She was so happy—and so tired. She kissed the fuzzy top of Nathan's head and let her body relax. She had nearly dozed off when a sudden idea hit her.

"Mrs. Taylorson," she asked sleepily, "would you be so kind as to have a telegram sent to my folks tomorrow?"

"Certainly, miss," the woman replied. "What would ya be wantin' it to say?" She took a paper and pencil from the desk and handed it to Missie. "Better write it down, in case I forget."

Missie thought for a few moments, then began to write slowly: "Nathan Isaiah arrived safely October 10 Stop Love from Missie and Baby." She handed the sheet to Mrs. Taylorson.

"It would pleasure me to be the bearer of such good news," she said with a warm pat on Missie's shoulder.

Missie smiled ruefully at the small bundle snuggled beside her. "If only there was some way to let his pa know. I'm going to have an awfully hard time waiting for the twenty-second. Why, Willie's son will be nigh grown-up by the time his pa gets to hold him!"

Mrs. Taylorson looked down at the tiny bundle on Missie's arm. "Seems to me," she smiled, "a little growin' time ain't gonna hurt the wee fella much. I don't reckon he's gonna out-grow thet little nightie he's a swimmin' in, in jest two weeks' time."

Missie smiled contentedly and let sleep claim her.

———

Willie drove into Tettsford Junction with the wagon on October twentieth, prepared for as many days of waiting as was necessary before welcoming his child. Mrs. Taylorson let him in the front door and managed, as promised, not to reveal the household's wonderful news. Willie went on up to Missie's room.

Missie was standing at her window looking wistfully out over the back garden at the distant hills. She was restless again, now that she was on her feet. Nathan, at this stage, seemed content to eat and sleep—and grow—daily, though he hadn't managed yet to fill out his nightie, just as Mrs. Taylorson had predicted. So Missie often felt at loose ends with time on her hands.

At the sound of the door, Missie did not even turn around. She had become accustomed to Mrs. Taylorson using any and every excuse to come in and out of the room. If she wasn't bringing Missie tea with lots of milk, she came just to check on the baby.

At Willie's alarmed "What's happened?" Missie whirled around.

"Willie!" she squealed.

He seemed paralyzed. "What's happened?" he repeated, fear in his voice.

"What do you mean, what's *happened?*"

Willie gestured speechlessly at Missie's trim figure, and she then realized why his face had gone white.

A smile spread over her face, and she rushed to fall into his arms.

"You're a pa! That's what's happened."

"Already?"

"He fooled us, didn't he?"

"He?"

"Look!"

Missie grasped Willie's hand and led him to the foot of the bed, where the small bundle lay peacefully sleeping in a simple cradle made by Mr. Weiss. One fist curled gently beside Nathan's full cheeks.

"Ours?" Willie whispered in awe.

"Ours," Missie said. "Isn't he wonderful?"

"Can we . . . can we git 'im out of there?" Willie asked. She could see him swallowing hard and blinking back tears. Missie nodded. Willie bent down and carefully picked up his son.

"Isn't he somethin' wonderful?" he repeated.

Missie could hardly hold all the joy she felt. Willie was here. Willie was pleased with his son—her gift to him. She reached up and kissed her husband's cheek, then leaned against his shoulder.

"I think he looks like his pa," she whispered, stroking the soft little cheek. "Look, he's going to have dark hair. Oh, I know he'll likely lose all the baby fuzz, but I think when it comes in again, it'll be dark like yours. And wait until he opens his eyes. They're blue now, but a dark, hazy blue. I'm thinking that before long they're going to be as brown as his pa's." Willie turned his head and bent to kiss Missie once more.

"But just look at this." Missie's voice held a hint of amazement and joy. She gently touched young Nathan on his soft chin. "A dimple! A dimple just like yours."

She expected a protest, but instead Willie looked at the small chin and grinned.

"Aw, c'mon," he said, but he wasn't expecting an argument.

The two sat down on the bed, the baby still in Willie's arms.

"When did he arrive?"

"October the tenth."

"The *tenth*? That's way early."

"He's almost two weeks old already—and ready to travel."

"Yer sure?"

"Doc says if we take it easy, we should be able to go most anytime."

Willie seemed too moved to answer.

"It won't take long, will it—to be ready to go?" Missie asked.

Willie shook his head and found his voice. "No . . . no, not long. I'll git right on it. Henry came with me this time. We brought two teams so's we'd have plenty of room fer supplies and not have to crowd ya none." He laughed. "Henry's gonna be a heap disappointed. We were all set fer a month-long stay."

Missie laughed quietly. "Oh, Willie, I can hardly wait. I'm so tired of being on my own in this town. I've been so lonesome."

The baby stirred, and Willie adjusted him in his arms.

"Hey," Willie said suddenly. "Has he got a name?"

"He has," Missie assured him, "and a good one, too. He's Nathan—Nathan Isaiah."

"Nathan Isaiah," Willie repeated. "I like it. I like it a lot." Lifting his small son up so he could plant a kiss on his downy head, he whispered, "Nathan Isaiah, I love you." The baby answered by wrinkling up his little face and letting out a lusty cry. His parents both laughed, and then Missie took him in hand to feed him.

After four days, the LaHayes were ready to leave. Mrs. Taylorson could hardly bear to see them go. She cooed and cuddled the baby and insisted upon holding him until the very last moment. Even Mr. Taylorson took time off from his store to come and see them off. He reminded them three times to consider their home as their own, should they be back in town.

Kathy and Melinda were both tearful, and they both brought going-away gifts for Baby Nathan. The kind old preacher offered a parting prayer, and his wife insisted they have some of her fresh-baked bread for the trail.

Henry fussed over Missie's bed in the wagon, determined that no wind or rain should be allowed to cause discomfort for her or the baby. It was not so hot for traveling now. In fact, Missie had to bundle up both herself and the baby against a cool breeze.

At last they were on the trail, and Missie mentally ticked off the *new* calendar she carried in her head. In just six days they would be *home*. Finally she would see the land Willie had learned to love. Her excitement grew within her until she could hardly contain it. At last she would be free of the drab, barren, dusty town. She would move into her own home like a nesting bird and make their dreams come true. She cradled her son close to her. "And you—you little rascal," she crooned to him, "you weren't even in those dreams. But I think you're going to fit in just fine."

SIXTEEN

The Ranch

"We're almost there now," Willie announced, excitement in his voice. "Jest over thet next hill."

They had already traveled six days. For fear of tiring Missie or the baby, Willie had stopped each evening a little earlier than would have been normal. Now it was noon of the seventh day.

Missie swallowed hard. Their very own homestead, their dream—Willie's and hers—was "just over the next hill." But the countryside they had been traveling through was even bleaker than that around Tettsford Junction. Until she saw some improvement in the landscape with her own eyes, Missie was finding it impossible to believe there would be any significant change. Hills and more colorless hills, covered only with coarse, dry-looking grass. Tumbleweeds somersaulted along in the wind, rolling and bouncing forever and ever. Occasional cactus plants or an outcropping of rocks were the only variations in the scenery. But maybe by some miracle . . . She so wanted to share Willie's enthusiasm.

Far in the distance was a line of dark mountains. Missie had expected—had hoped—that the mountains would become her friends. But they remained aloof, offering only a dim outline, shadowing themselves in a gloomy haze.

"Sometimes they're purple—sometimes blue—sometimes almost pink," Willie had explained, "dependin' on how the sun hits 'em. An' then in the winter, with the snow on their peaks, they're a dazzle of white."

"Can we see the mountains from our place?" Missie had asked, fervently hoping it might be so. She was eager to enjoy Willie's mountains in each of their changing moods.

"Not from our valley," Willie had responded. "In order to see the mountains ya'd have to build up on a hill—an' ya wouldn't want thet. Too much wind, no protection."

"Too much wind," Missie murmured softly now, thinking back on Willie's words. "Way too much wind." She wrapped her heavy shawl more tightly about her against its steady blowing.

So they couldn't see the mountains from their house. Then what *could* they see? She had asked Willie that, too.

"Lookin' to the east, down the draw," Willie had told her, "ya can look right out on the range. Mile after mile of low hills, with nothin' to git in the way of yer lookin'." Willie seemed to feel those empty miles to gaze upon were a great asset. What Missie pictured in her mind's eye made her shiver.

They now topped the hill, and Willie reined in the team. Missie shut her eyes, wishing she didn't have to open them just yet.

"Well," Willie announced triumphantly, "there it is. Ain't it somethin'?"

Missie opened her eyes slowly.

Tucked in a small valley, just as Willie had said, were a few small scattered structures and what seemed like miles and miles of corral fence.

"You said it was *green,*" Missie said through stiff lips, immediately regretting the remark.

"It is in the springtime. This is late fall. Nothin's green now." Willie remained unshaken. "Well, what d'ya think of it?"

Missie had been dreading that question. How could she

answer it? She couldn't let Willie down—yet she couldn't lie.

"It's . . . it's . . . really something," she managed, thankful she had remembered Willie's own words.

"Sure is," Willie agreed, obviously interpreting her answer with his own optimism.

He pointed a finger toward the valley and leaned toward her.

"The corrals for the horses and cows all lay over there."

Missie fleetingly wondered how he ever thought she or anyone else could miss them. They seemed to fill up the whole valley.

Willie continued, "Thet there buildin' is the barn. We'll build an even bigger one later. Thet there's the bunkhouse right in there, an' the cook shack is there beside it."

"Where's the house?" asked Missie.

"The *temporary* one? Right there."

Missie's eyes followed his finger. The *temporary* house, like the bunkhouse, cook shack, and barn, looked to her like a giant heap of dried grass.

"They're made of sod," Willie informed her matter-of-factly.

"Sod?"

"Yeah. Ya cut blocks of sod from the ground an' pile 'em up. Makes a real snug place to live in fer the winter."

Missie swallowed, eyes staring and heart pounding. "Sod," she whispered. Her lips trembled as she fought to control her emotions, and she turned her face away.

Willie spoke to the team and the wagon rumbled on. Missie closed her eyes again. No miracle had taken place "over the next hill." There was no fairyland awaiting her. But she needed a miracle now—to help her through the ordeal she knew lay ahead.

The sod house at a distance had been shock enough, but Missie's close-up view of it was even more difficult. As the wagon creaked to a stop before the small, low structure, Missie caught her lip between her teeth to keep a sob from escaping.

Henry had arrived earlier and started a fire to warm the house for the baby. He emerged now, grinning eagerly from ear to ear.

The smoke poured from the little pipe of a chimney and dissipated into the wind. Missie recognized the pungent odor of buffalo chips. They had been forced many times on the trail to use them when wood supplies had been scarce, but Missie had never really accepted or appreciated this type of fuel. As she sat on the wagon seat, she looked around and realized that there would be no wood. There were few trees in sight.

Willie helped her down and she stood a moment to steady her legs and her mind, bracing herself for whatever she found behind the dwarfed door that guarded the entrance to her new home.

Willie led the way, and Missie ducked her head to follow him into the dark interior of the little sod house.

It was high noon, and still the room was so dark Missie's eyes took several moments to adjust. When she finally could see, she gazed around the one small room. In the corner was their bed, but not the neat, spread-covered version she had pictured. It was an oversized platform with a quilt hastily thrown over some kind of lumpy bedding—definitely made up by a man.

A small black stove hovered beneath the smoke-spewing chimney. Close beside it were a small wooden table and two stools pushed beneath it. A cluttered shelf stretched along the wall, with crocks and tins randomly stacked across it.

The two tiny windows were hardly large enough to look out of—and one had to stoop to do so. The small panes of dirty glass were held snugly in place by the sod stacked firmly around them. Missie, her thoughts swirling around like leaves in a wind, promised herself she would give them a good washing at her first opportunity. She jerked her thoughts away from the windows, amazed that at such a traumatic moment she could even notice the dirt on the tiny panes.

Her gaze traveled up to the ceiling. It, too, was sod held precariously in place by strips of board, twine, and wire. It looked as if it periodically gave up parts of itself. Would it come tumbling down—on her, on her baby?

She quickly lowered her eyes lest they give her away—and immediately noticed the floor. It was dirt! Hard-packed, uneven dirt. Missie sucked in a ragged breath, but Willie was talking cheerily.

"It ain't much, but it's warm an' snug. Come next year we'll build a *real* house—of either rock or wood—ya can have yer choice."

"Coffee's ready," Henry called. Willie stepped forward to take Nathan from Missie. She was reluctant to let him go but gradually released her grip, and Willie put him down on the bed. Her eyes surveyed the roof above the bed to be sure a clump of turf was not about to fall.

"Sit right here," Henry invited, and Missie numbly did as she was told.

The hot coffee revived her somewhat, and Missie soon discovered that her hands and feet could move again. She felt Henry's eyes upon her and knew she must respond in some way.

"Well," she said, forcing a chuckle past the lump in her throat, "sure won't be much to keeping house." She saw Henry's face relax.

Willie reached for her hand. "I know it won't be easy, Missie—this first year—but jest you wait. Next year, I promise, we'll build ya jest what ya want."

Missie took another swallow of coffee. Henry had brewed it strong and dark. Oh, how she needed its strength right now.

"Where are all the crates and boxes of my things?" she asked softly. She was surprised she had said the word *my,* but she couldn't have avoided it.

"We stored 'em in the back shed by the barn until ya got here. We didn't rightly know jest which stuff you'd want. I can git 'em fer ya right away, iffen you'd like."

Missie looked around her at the already crowded room.

"I think you'd best leave them where they are for now. There doesn't seem to be much room for extras here. And, Willie, put my sewing machine with them, too, will you please?"

Willie started to argue, but then his eyes also surveyed the room.

"Does seem a mite crowded like," he said. "Funny, it seemed plumb empty when you were gone."

"Yer team is still standin' out there," Henry broke in, placing his cup on the table. "I think thet I'd best go on out an' take care of 'em. Where d'ya want the wagon left?"

"Jest pull it up beside the house. We still have to move in all the things fer this young'un."

Henry nodded and left.

"Where's Henry stayin'?" Missie asked, toying with her cup.

"In the bunkhouse."

"Alone?"

"No, we have three others there now. Two hands an' the cook."

"Must be crowded."

"They don't have much gear."

"You've got more cattle, then?"

"A nice start."

"And horses?"

"A fairly good string."

"You're about fixed, then, I imagine."

Willie nodded slowly, pushed his cup back, and rubbed his hands over his weary-looking face. He stood and walked to the window, bending his head to look out at whatever lay beyond.

"Missie," he said without turning around, "this was a mistake. Don't know why I didn't see it before. Jest too plumb lonesome to think straight, I guess. I never shoulda brought ya here. I shoulda left ya there at Tettsford till I had a decent house built. This ain't no fittin' place fer a woman . . . an' a baby."

Missie went silently to him, terribly sorry her feelings had been so transparent. It must have hurt Willie to see her disappointment.

"Oh, Willie," she said reaching her arms around his neck and pulling his head down toward her. "It's all right. Truly it is. I admit, it did catch me off guard, but I'll get used to it. Really. Really I will. I'd have never stayed there in Tettsford—not without you. I was so lonesome for you I nearly died of it every day. I'd as soon be here—no, *sooner*—I'd *sooner* be here with you than back there in that bedroom all alone."

Willie pulled her tight. "Missie, I'm sorry . . . sorry," he whispered, "but it won't always be this way. I promise. I'll make it up to ya someday. Jest as soon as I can. Ya'll have jest as fine a place as yer own home was . . . as ya deserve to have."

My home! Missie thought, closing her eyes. *Oh, if only I were at home!* Wasn't that where she really belonged? Why hadn't Willie been content with it, too?

She looked across at the sleeping baby and the tears stung her eyes. Willie was kissing the top of her head. If she could keep from looking up at him, she could recover her composure. Nathan began to fuss, and Missie turned gently from Willie without lifting her face.

Taking a breath to steady her voice, she said, "He's hungry. Guess I'd better care for him before I do anything else."

"I'll bring in his things," Willie said and reached for his hat. "Missie." He stopped at the door and turned to her. "I love you."

She looked at him, nodded, and forced a smile before he went out the door.

I'd sooner be here with you than back there in that bedroom all alone, she repeated over and over again.

SEVENTEEN

Winter and Christmas

Missie lifted the already heavy buckets and trudged forward a few paces. She dropped them with a thump and stooped again to gather buffalo chips from the near-frozen ground. The driving wind whipped her shawl, and she made an effort to wrap it more securely about her. Her fingers tingled from the cold. She chided herself for not having worn mittens.

At length the second pail was full. She hoisted her load and hiked slowly back to her sod house, the buckets thumping against her legs. She would need two more pails to complete the day's supply. She dreaded the thought of going out once more. Her arms and back were aching, and she was now having to range farther and farther from the house in order to fill the pails.

As she neared the soddy she could hear little Nathan crying. She hurried her steps. Poor little fellow! How long had he been asking for his dinner?

Missie set down her load, then scrubbed her hands thoroughly at the basin in the corner. The cold water increased the tingling feeling, and she rubbed them vigorously with the rough towel in an effort to restore the proper circulation. At last there was feeling in her fingers again. Casting her shawl aside, she hurried to her baby, crooning words of love to him even before she reached his bed.

Somehow she had managed two long weeks of living in the crowded soddy. Nathan was a big part of the reason she was able to function at all. The wee baby brought life and meaning to Missie's world, such as it was.

The air was growing colder now and the wind more harsh. Willie's eyes, full of concern, often watched the sky. A winter storm of sleet and snow could sweep in upon them long before he and his farmhands were ready for it. Missie worried about her dwindling fuel supply, but she said nothing to Willie. No need to give him further worries. Surely a woman should be able to shoulder the task of keeping the fire going. Still, she didn't know how she would manage it once the snow covered the ground. Frets about that and other matters related to simply surviving nagged constantly in the back of her mind.

She changed Nathan, fed him, and held him close for several minutes before returning him to his bed.

Missie checked the coffeepot on her small stove. The full-sized stove she had brought from "back home" at her mama's insistence remained packed in its crate. It was too big for the little sod house. Missie pushed the kettle toward the center so the water would boil. Willie might soon be in, and he would be chilled to the bone. But it was Henry's voice Missie heard first, just outside the door.

"Still think thet we can't put it off any longer—no matter what else needs to be done. Snow could come anytime."

"Yeah," Willie agreed, "yer right. Shouldn'ta let it go this long. We'll plan on first thing in the mornin'. We'll use two wagons an' all the hands."

"Ya think they'll mind?"

"I'm boss, ain't I?"

"Sure ya are."

Missie could sense the grin in Henry's voice.

"But I reckon they might think they was hired on to punch cows—not pick up chips."

"We'll see," Willie said as the two men ducked through the door.

Oh, Missie thought, *if only this means what I hope it means.*

The next morning, soon after breakfast, two wagons and five men set out to gather chips for the winter fires. All day long they shuttled back and forth. They heaped the cook's supply beside the cook shack but favored Missie with more consideration. Her pile was stored in a sod shed just behind the house. This would save her the struggle of breaking frozen chips out of the snow.

Missie nearly cried with relief as she watched the shed fill up. Gathering chips would have been an increasingly difficult task with the coming of the winter snows. *Thank you, God,* her heart whispered. "And thank you, Willie—and all of you," she would say to each of them as she was able. Missie felt light with her gratefulness. She groped for a way to express her deep appreciation. At the same time she reached for her large coffeepot and filled it to the brim. She'd at least have steaming coffee waiting to warm the men on their next trip in.

The next day the men continued hauling, and even the next—piling the overflow beside the shed. To Missie it looked like the supply would last forever. It did to some of the hands, also, if their mutters and scowls were any indication. But Willie declared he wanted to be absolutely sure his wife had plenty on hand for warm fires throughout the coming winter.

Missie's days became easier after the chips had been gathered. But her time was also more difficult to fill with activity. The little room needed very little attention. Missie made attempts at sweeping the floor, made up the bed, prepared the meals, and washed the dishes. Of course, she often had to make a trip to the spring when she ran out of water, which Willie hauled for her before leaving for his daily duties. Beyond that, there wasn't much to fill her hours.

She decided to knit socks for Henry—then continued to knit a pair for each of the ranch hands. She would have them ready for Christmas. After the socks were finished and Missie's idle hands lay useless in her lap once again, she decided to make each of the men heavy woolen mittens for the winter days ahead. She hesitated—not sure if cowboys would scorn such things as woolen mittens, but eventually she proceeded anyway.

Missie did not know the men well. The tall, lean, hard-faced one with the large nose was Clem. The shorter tobacco-spitting one was Sandy. Missie was a bit more familiar with Cookie—the cook, of course. He was a quiet but pleasant man whose sharp eyes seemingly missed nothing. His face was plain until lit with a smile—which occurred whenever he saw Missie or her small son. Cookie suffered with a bad limp, the reason he was content to cook rather than ride the range with the other men. A bad fall while breaking a horse was his explanation for the faulty hip and leg. Missie was glad he was around, for though they rarely conversed, his occasional nod and grin brightened her day a bit.

The baby's laundry was Missie's most trying task. The water had to be hauled from the spring below the house. Though Willie filled the two available pails before he left in the morning, it wasn't nearly enough for Missie to do the job. The little stove was too small to hold a tub or a boiler, so Missie had to heat the water kettle by kettle. By the time she had the next kettleful hot, the first one had cooled. Having been raised to wash clothes in *hot* water, she found her patience sorely tested.

The first winter storm attacked with fury. Driving wind whipped the cutting sleet, smashing it against the small windows, swirling it around each corner of the sod house. The snow stacked in drifts and buried any obstacle in its pathway. Missie prayed that their little soddy would be able to withstand the storm's anger.

Willie insisted on being out with the men and animals, and Missie felt it was only sensible for him to be *in*. All hands rode throughout the day to insure that the three hundred cattle now wearing the *Hanging W* brand were not lost in the storm.

They returned late in the afternoon, having hazed the cattle into a box-canyon, which they hoped would offer some protection from the worst of the weather.

Still, Willie fretted and paced, ducking down to watch the driving snow through the small pane of window glass.

The storm had lost some of its fury by the next afternoon, and Henry and Sandy rode out to check the stock. They were able to report back that all were accounted for. Willie relaxed again.

The snow did not melt away, and Missie realized that winter was not about to retreat. The spring soon froze, and Missie was forced to melt snow for their water supply. It was a tedious task, particularly on washdays. She didn't care for the taste of snow water, either, but gradually adjusted to it.

Missie found her life to be uneventful, repetitious, boring. The deep drifts all about the little sod house blocked her view of even those empty frost-painted hills. The tasks of bringing in fuel for her fire and melting enough snow to keep water in the house provided Missie with nothing except *work*.

How glad Missie was for Nathan. As he became aware of what was happening around him and his smile greeted Missie when she looked over at him in his bed, her days took on some meaning and purpose. She talked to him constantly. Without him, the dark walls of the tiny soddy would have been a prison during those long, empty wintry days.

"Thank you, Father," Missie prayed often. "Thank you for our son. And help me to be cheerful and patient and to make a happy home for Willie," she added.

As Missie hung the baby's laundry from the lines strung across their one room, she suddenly realized that only a few days remained until Christmas.

She ducked under a line of hanging diapers and made her way to another homemade calendar clipped on the wall. It was true. There were only four days until Christmas.

She looked about her. Christmas? Here? She shook her head quickly to blink away threatening tears and scolded herself. But the aching feeling within her was not to be shaken off so easily. What could she possibly do to make this soddy ready for Christmas?

That evening as she and Willie sat at their small table to eat their stew and biscuits, Missie brought up the subject.

"Did you realize that in just four days it's Christmas?"

"Christmas?" Willie said, looking surprised. "Christmas already? Boy, how time does fly!"

Missie felt a sharp retort forming on her tongue, but she refused to voice it.

"Christmas!" Willie repeated. "I can hardly believe it."

He finished the biscuit. "Guess I can't provide ya with a turkey. Will a roast of venison do?"

"I think so. Maybe Cookie can tell me how to fix it."

"Be kinda hard havin' Christmas alone, won't it?" Willie's eyes searched her face carefully.

"I've been thinking about it," Missie said. "Why don't we have the hands in?"

"In *here*?"

"Why not?"

Willie stared at the lines of hanging baby things. "Not much room."

"I know, but we could make do."

"They could come two at a time, I guess."

"That wouldn't be *Christmas*."

"How'll ya do it, then?"

"I'll set the food out on the table and the stove, and we'll just help ourselves and sit wherever we fit—on the stools, on the bed—wherever. I think there's one more stool in the bunkhouse—and Cookie has one in the cook shack."

Willie laughed. "You've got yer heart set on it, ain't ya?"

Missie lowered her head but made no comment.

"Okay," said Willie, "invite the men."

"Would you invite them, please, Willie? I . . . I don't see them much."

"Sure, I'll invite 'em. Fer what time?"

"Let's make it one o'clock."

Willie nodded. "An' I'll git ya thet venison roast."

"Maybe Cookie could do the roast in his stove. Then I can have mine free for other things."

Willie nodded again. "I'll talk to 'im."

Cookie agreed to do the roast, and when the day arrived, Missie got busy on the remainder of the meal. She didn't have much to work with, but what she lacked in ingredients, she made up for with ingenuity. She had been hoarding some of her mother's preserves for just such a time as this. She opened them now and used some of the fruit to fill tart shells. She prepared some of the last canned carrots and beans from home to go with the roast venison. The only potatoes left were a few precious ones that she had kept, hoping to plant them in the spring. They looked sorry and neglected, but Missie still prayed they might have the germ of life left in them. She refused to use any of them now, although the thought of potatoes with the meal made her mouth water. Instead, she baked a big batch of fluffy biscuits and set out her last jar of honey to go with them.

When the men arrived, Cookie proudly carrying his roast of venison, Missie was ready for them.

"Before we eat," Willie said, "I've somethin' else to bring in. We don't have much room, iffen ya noticed"—this brought a guffaw from the men—"so I left it in the other shed."

He soon returned carrying a scrub bush, held upright in a small pail. On its tiny branches hung little bows made from Missie's scraps of yarn.

"Didn't rightly seem like Christmas without a tree," he said apologetically. The men whooped, and Missie wept.

When the commotion had died down, Willie moved with some difficulty to the middle of the room and led them in prayer: "Father, we have much to thank you fer. Fer the good-smellin' food of which we are about to partake. Fer the warmth of this little room in which we are to share it. Fer friends who are here with us an' those who are far away. Fer the memories of other Christmases spent with those we love. Fer Nathan Isaiah, our healthy son. And most of all, dear God, fer my wife, who has blessed us all by givin' us this Christmas. We are reminded thet all of these blessin's are extras. Yer special gift to us on this day was yer Son. We accept thet gift with our thanks. Amen."

———

As the menfolk devoured the tasty and plentiful food, Missie sat quietly. She tried to keep her thoughts from wandering to her parents' home. What would it be like if she could be there right now? In a house big enough to serve a whole family in comfort, with fresh butter, mashed potatoes, turkey, baked squash, and apple pie topped with whipped cream.

She looked at her plate filled with sliced venison and gravy, canned carrots with no garnish, canned yellow beans, and a biscuit with no butter. But she reminded herself that many days during the last year she had partaken of even simpler fare. This was a rather sumptuous feast by comparison. The men obviously felt it was such. And when it came time for the tarts and coffee, they licked their lips in anticipation. Missie picked her way across the room to check on Nathan. One could barely move without tripping over feet, but the close proximity just made it easier for laughing together.

"Son," she whispered to the baby, "you're not going to remember one thing about this, but I want you to get in on it anyway. Your very first Christmas, and I don't even have anything to give you—but a kiss and laughter with friends." She took him in her arms.

After the meal Missie summoned all her courage and presented each of the men with a pair of socks and woolen mittens. She was unprepared for their deep appreciation. She soon realized that it may have been their first Christmas gift since they were small boys at home.

Cookie shifted his position to "git outta the smoke from the blasted fire—it's makin' my eyes water."

Clem swallowed over and over, his Adam's apple lurching up and down.

Missie prayed that none of them would feel embarrassed at having nothing to give in return.

After the men had expressed their thanks as best as they could, Missie began timidly, "Now I want to say thank you for your gift to me."

Five pairs of eyes—six, counting Nathan's—swung to her face.

"I want to thank you," she said shyly, "for working so faithfully for my husband, for making his load—and thus mine—easier, for not demanding things that we can't provide." She hesitated, then added, smiling, "But most of all, I want to thank you for the good supply of chips you didn't fuss about hauling. I've been thankful over and over for those chips."

Missie couldn't suppress a giggle. Though the expressions of the men acknowledged her sincere thankfulness, they also saw the humor in it and gladly chuckled with her.

Though unaware of it at that moment, Missie had just made some friends for life. Not one of those men sitting round her tiny soddy would have denied her anything that was in their power to provide. There she sat, just a little scrap of a girl-woman, youthful and pretty, her cheeks glowing with health, her eyes sparkling near tears, her trim figure clothed attractively in a bright calico, the tiny fair-skinned, chubby-cheeked Nathan contentedly in her arms studying her face.

That picture was their Christmas gift, one they would remember all their lives.

Later Henry brought in his guitar, and they sang Christmas carols together. Cookie just sat and listened. Sandy whistled a few lines now and then. But Clem, to Missie's surprise, seemed to know most of the traditional carols by heart.

It was hard to break up the little gathering. Several times Missie added more chips to her fire. Little Nathan made the rounds from one pair of arms to another. Even the tough-looking Clem took a turn holding the baby.

At last Missie put the coffeepot back on and boiled a fresh pot. She was glad she had made enough tarts for each of them to have another one with their coffee.

The men lingered over their tarts and coffee but finally

took their leave, tramping their way through the snow back to the bunkhouse.

Missie hummed softly as she washed the dishes. There had been no point trying to find room to wash them earlier. Willie put on his hat and coat and left for the barn to check the horses, Missie assumed.

Missie had finished the dishes and was feeding Nathan when Willie returned, bearing a box. Missie was astonished, and he answered her unasked question.

"I did my Christmas shopping 'fore we left Tettsford." He set his box on the table and began to unpack it.

" 'Fraid my gift don't seem too fittin' like in these surroundin's. I was sorta seein' it in our *real* house when I bought it, I guess. Anyway, I thought thet I'd show it to ya, an' then we can sorta pack it off again." Willie lifted from the box the most beautiful fruit bowl Missie had ever seen.

She gasped, "Willie! It's beautiful."

Willie looked very relieved when he saw the bowl had brought her pleasure. He set it gently on the table.

"I'll let ya git a better look at it when yer done with Nathan. Then I'll pack it on back—out of yer way."

"Oh no," Missie protested. "Just leave it here. Please."

She laid the baby on the bed and went to the table to pick up the bowl. "It's lovely," she said, her fingers caressing it. "Thank you, Willie."

She reached up to kiss him. "And I don't want you to pack it away. It'll be a reminder . . . and a promise. I . . . I need it here. Don't you see?"

Willie held her close. "I see."

After a moment of silence, Willie spoke softly. "Missie, I wonder . . . I wonder iffen you'll ever know jest how happy ya made five people today?"

"Five?"

"Those four cowpokes . . . an' *me*."

Missie's heart was full, and she smiled.

"Then make it *six*, Willie . . . because in doing what I could, the pleasure all poured right back on me. And I got the biggest helping of happiness myself!"

EIGHTEEN

Missie's New Home

After the anticipation and preparation for Christmas and the joyful celebration it turned out to be, the winter days fell back into their previous monotony. At times Missie felt she could endure no more, confined as she was in the cramped, stuffy soddy. Her only company for most of her days was Baby Nathan. She wondered if she might spoil him with all the attention he received. It was a good thing he fussed very little, for Missie used every little cry or murmur as an excuse to pamper and cuddle him. He responded with toothless smiles and waving fists.

When he slept, Missie tried her best to find other things to keep herself busy. If there was laundry to do, that could take most of a morning, leaving dripping clothing hanging around the already crowded room. But it was satisfying to have clean garments ready to wear. Of course clean diapers for Nathan were a daily chore. Occasionally there was wild game that one of the men had brought in, and after it had been butchered and dressed, she would prepare her and Willie's portion in stews or panfry it. But most days' meals meant very simple fare and did not require much time to make.

She no longer had to make those daily treks to the fuel shack—ever since Christmas, a good supply of chips appeared beside her door every day before she had even climbed out of bed. Missie never discovered which one of the men delivered them.

She had no room for books except the Bible she and Willie read from each morning after breakfast. Her hands had long since run out of materials for crafts and activities to occupy them, and the walls of the room seemed to press ever more closely about her.

Baby Nathan gained weight, gurgled and cooed, and tried to chew everything his small hands could get to his mouth. It became more and more difficult to find a safe place to leave the wee child, who could now scoot to the edge of the bed. She couldn't put him on the dirt floor to roll around, and she had to watch him carefully when she put him on the bed for his playtimes.

Though time with his son was limited by the demands of the ranch, Willie also doted on little Nathan. Missie sometimes teased that if it had not been for the baby, Willie would have been content to live out with his precious cows! When Nathan began to squeal at the sight of his daddy and laugh at their roughhouse play, Willie found it more difficult to say good-bye and leave the house to go back to the men and the stock.

Missie was gazing out the tiny window with glimmers of hope that the worst of the winter was over when a sudden angry-sounding wind swept in from the north. It caught the crew off guard, and before the men could even saddle up to go look after the cows, the snow came—swishing, blinding clouds of it seemed set on devouring everything in its path. Willie realized it was foolhardy to send men out in such a storm. He would just have to leave the animals on their own and hope they could find some shelter.

The storm moved on after two days. By then the drifts of snow had piled high all around. The soddy's door was almost buried by the whiteness. Willie had to wait for the ranch hands to dig him out.

All were finally able to leave their quarters, and the men quickly saddled up to go out looking for the range cattle in the hills. After combing the area for three days, the reports were heartbreaking. At least seventy-five head of cattle had been lost in the storm. Missie wept. Willie tried to assure her they'd make out fine, that temporary setbacks were to be expected. But she could see a troubled look in his eyes. They both turned again to their Isaiah passage for comfort and strength.

At the end of February one of the milk cows calved, and Missie felt as though she had been handed an unimaginable treasure. Even the loss of the cattle the week before was put from her mind. With milk on hand, what wonderful possibilities she could imagine for improving their diet!

"What I couldn't do now if I just had some eggs," she told Willie. She promised herself that as soon as possible she'd do something about that.

———————

Spring eventually did come—slowly, almost imperceptibly, until one morning Missie was confident there was a faint warmth in the air. The drifts of snow began to shrink, and gradually dark spots of earth appeared. The spring started to trickle again and the stubby bushes beside it dressed themselves in a shy green.

Missie secretly mourned for the sight of budding trees, of blossoming shrubs, but only empty hills stretched away from her gaze. To her great joy, a few wild flowers timidly made their appearance. Missie couldn't resist picking some to grace her table. In the dimness of the little sod house, one had to bend over the tin cup that held the flowers in order to fully appreciate the tiny bits of color. But just knowing they were there helped to lift her spirits.

As the snow receded, the men spent much more time out on the range, watching the cattle vigilantly. Spring calves were arriving daily. They would not totter about many days before the *Hanging W,* Willie's brand, would show on their flanks.

Missie wasn't particularly happy about the name attached to Willie's ranch, not in favor of "hanging" even a *W.* But Willie laughed at her squeamishness. All of their stock bore the brand.

Willie told her that the hard range riding of spring roundup was beginning. Day after day the men would ride, gathering the scattered stock and their calves. They would all be driven to the wide box-canyon where they had been protected during the first winter storm, he explained before kissing his son and Missie good-bye for a few days.

When the roundup was completed, the men counted one hundred ninety-eight head of cattle and one hundred six calves.

"Even with the last storm," Willie maintained, "thet's a few more'n we started with."

The wagons were moved out to the canyon to serve as bunkhouses during the spring branding. Cookie slept in the chow wagon, as well as using it for kitchen, supply shack, and blacksmith shop.

The men were divided into shifts for the night hours, and Willie and Sandy took the first watch.

It wasn't long until the cattle adjusted to their more confined surroundings. The lowing and milling subsided, and they bedded down for the night.

After midnight Henry and Clem took over the night-watch duties. Sandy and Willie gladly unsaddled their mounts and cozied up to Cookie's open fire. They drank mugs of hot coffee to warm their bones before trying to get a few hours of sleep. The early morning sun would soon summon them to another busy day with the branding irons.

Shortly before daybreak a commotion among the herd got Henry's and Clem's attention, but they could not quickly pinpoint the source of the sudden restlessness and shifting of the herd.

By the time they realized the cause, a band of rustlers was driving off a large portion of the herd. Henry and Clem rode hard, but in spite of their best efforts they were able to cut back only the stragglers from the stampeding cattle. No shots had been fired, but Henry and Clem had counted, in spite of the darkness and confusion, at least five rustlers. By the time the sleeping men in the wagons heard the ruckus and recognized what it was, it was too late for them to assist.

The next morning the discouraged men ranged out farther, gathering the few head that had somehow eluded the rustlers. After all the cattle in their possession had been gathered and counted, Willie found that his herd now numbered only fifty-four head of full-grown cattle and thirty-two calves.

After the final count, Willie turned away in defeat. He had known all along that he would suffer some losses to weather and rustlers, but he had dared to hope that the numbers would be few and over a longer period of time. *Why,* he asked himself, *why did I think we would be spared when so many other ranchers have been completely wiped out? I should feel lucky to have any cattle left— any at all.*

Willie swallowed the hard lump in his throat and lifted his broad-brimmed hat to wipe the dust from his brow. The sick feeling in the pit of his stomach refused to leave. Could he get back on his feet? How long would it take? If he had been more patient and had worked for another year before coming out to his ranch, he could have laid aside enough cash to cover such a tragic setback.

Now the only cash he had on hand was the money for Missie's house. How could he ever tell her? Even now he could picture those frank blue eyes, intense with hurt and fright and disappointment from the news.

Though he wished with every ounce of his being he could do so, he knew it would be useless and untruthful to try to keep it from her. She deserved to know the facts—even to know the seriousness of their situation. But Willie determined that in every way possible he would try to shield her from the pain and fear that came with the knowing.

———————

When Willie presented Missie with the facts, she could tell he was explaining the situation as honestly and simply as he knew how. He talked as though this was inevitable—the loss of some cattle. But deep down, Missie knew better. She ached for him. If only there was some way she could help him.

Then within her breast arose a tiny surge of hope. Maybe now he would be satisfied to have tried his dream and be content to go back home. But very soon she knew Willie had no such intention. Instead, to Missie's surprise, he told his men that as soon as the work could be started, they would begin building the permanent ranch house.

Missie said nothing until they were alone that night. She began very carefully, "I overheard you discussing with the hands your plans for building."

"Yeah, iffen it's gonna be ready as planned, we need to get started."

"But, Willie," Missie protested softly. "Can we manage it now? Can we afford it?"

"What're ya meanin'?"

"Well, with the cattle losses and all."

"Thet changes nothin'. The money for the house has been set aside."

"But what about rebuilding the herd?"

"Thet'll jest have to wait."

"But can it? I mean, if we don't have a herd, there won't be cattle to sell, and if—"

"There'll be some . . . eventually. And I promised ya a house. We can't do both, Missie . . . an' the house comes first."

"Willie, listen." Missie was afraid she might later regret what she was about to say. But she had to say it. "Willie, I know about your promise. I know you want to keep it . . . and you will. But it could be postponed, Willie, for just a bit . . . until . . . until we have the cattle to sell. If we stay in this house, just for now, and use the put-aside money to help rebuild the herd, then next year . . . well, we could build our house then."

Missie saw Willie's jaw muscles tighten as if he was fighting for control.

"Please, Willie," she coaxed. "The cattle are important to *me*, too, you know."

"But ya couldn't keep on livin' here, not fer another whole year . . . another winter."

"Yes, I could," she hurried on with as much conviction as she could muster. "I'm getting used to it now. It's not very big, but it's warm. And now that spring is here, Nathan and I can go outside more. By fall he'll be walking. We'll manage. Honest!"

Silence followed. For a time Missie wondered if she had been refused. She didn't know whether to feel relieved or sorry. The house was small and difficult. Yet she knew if Willie was intending to stay here and ranch—and it seemed that indeed he was—then he needed to rebuild that herd. Without it their future was very insecure.

Her love for Willie drove her to decide for his happiness. She knew now he'd never be content to simply admit defeat, to leave his beloved hills and valleys, and return back east.

Oh, God, she prayed silently, *help me support Willie in spite of what I want. Keep your promise to uphold me now.*

Missie felt peace go through her being. The next thing she knew, Willie was pulling her close. She understood Willie was accepting her gift of postponement on the house in order to rebuild his herd. She reached her hand up to touch his cheeks and felt the tears. Her Willie was crying. She cried, too, but their shared emotions drew them even closer to each other.

NINETEEN

Missie's Garden

With the smell of spring in the air, Missie found herself even more restless as she anxiously waited for the final disappearance of snow. Nathan, increasingly active now, needed room in which to explore, and that would require the outdoors. Missie dared not leave him in the small sod house longer than a dash out back for more chips or to scoop up a pail of snow for her water supply.

She had tired of the melted snow for her water supply, but she did not feel it was any longer safe for her to make the trek to the trickling spring and leave the baby alone in the house, and she certainly could not carry him and a bucket of water, too. But logic did not keep her from *wanting* to go to the spring. Just the sight of its running water would be confirmation to her that spring was truly here.

She desperately needed to escape the four tight walls. She also needed a change of activity. Her fingers felt heavy and numb from hours of knitting and sewing. She was just plain bored—fed up with nearly everything that could be done in one small room.

Missie looked out on the sparkling day and, as many times in the past, wished with all her heart that she had some excuse to be out in the sunshine. If only she could saddle a horse and go out onto the prairies like the menfolk did. But with no one to leave small Nathan with, the idea was not workable.

Or is it?

Missie suddenly recalled a nostalgic item she had slipped into one of the boxes when packing. Before they left on their long trip west, she had found it tucked in the back of a drawer at home, and with tear-filled eyes, she had smuggled it in among some blankets. To another's eyes it would just have seemed like some kind of strange contraption, but to Missie it was *love* wrapped up in one simple, practical piece of equipment. Though Missie had no recollection of being carried in the backpack, her mama had long ago showed it to her and explained how her pa had lovingly fashioned it in order to carry her with him after she, just a tiny girl, had lost her first mother. He had never left her at home alone while he plowed his fields and did his choring until Marty joined the little family. Missie ran to the storage shed in her eagerness. With the backpack, she would be able to take that horseback ride, and the baby would be able to join her!

Once she had located the backpack and shown it to Willie, he selected a gentle mare and made her available to Missie whenever she wished to ride. Now she had something to look forward to when the weather cooperated. Even with the backpack, though, she could not ride far before Baby Nathan became too heavy, and Missie would reluctantly return to the little soddy. But she also used it to take him with her to the spring for fresh water.

Missie was bored with the sameness of the food she had to prepare every day. Nothing tasted good anymore—nothing was fresh. "Canned, dried, and bland" described everything. Her precious herbs and spices were carefully parceled out, since she didn't know when they could be replaced. She wondered if Willie found the meals as unpalatable as she did. But, of course,

Willie was too much of a gentleman to comment in any way but positively.

It seemed to Missie's worn, restless spirit that planting a garden would revive her again—and so she paced back and forth, willing the snow to go away. When fresh flurries sent scattered flakes whirling through the still crisp air, Missie wiped tears of disappointment on her apron.

Finally the snow flurries changed to rain showers, and Missie's hopes grew.

The snow melted reluctantly—especially where it had drifted by the spring. And that was the very location Missie wanted for her garden. She felt sorely tempted to go out with a shovel but checked herself from such foolish use of time and energy. The snow gradually lost the battle, and one day when Missie went to check she was surprised and thrilled to find all traces of the winter's cold and ice gone. She began hinting to Willie that he put a plow to the sod. Willie showed more patience than Missie.

"It's a bit early yet," he insisted. "The ground hasn't had a fair chance to warm. An' remember, this ain't the East. We're right close to the mountains here, an' frosts still come on the early spring nights."

But Missie could not bear the thought of being detained. Willie, realizing what it meant to her, relented and plowed the spot, though he shook his head at rushing the season like this.

Missie felt released from captivity as she sorted her seeds and set off for planting. She took a blanket on which to deposit Nathan, and set to work. She was sure the baby would be as joyful as she at finally being free from the four walls of the soddy, but he looked about in a perplexed manner and began to fuss. Missie tried to amuse him, but he continued to wail. She then turned him over onto his tummy and patted him gently until he fell asleep. At least the fresh air would do him good.

"You're missing so much by sleeping right now, my boy," she whispered. "The clear blue sky, the feel of the spring air, the smell of the soil. I do hope that someday you appreciate it all. But for now, your mama will just enjoy it for you."

Missie went to her planting. She was so glad she had plenty of seed. She was hungry in both body and soul for green growing things. Her impatience mounted with each seed she dropped into the ground. She could almost smell the vegetables cooking on her stove in the days ahead. The imagined taste and tang of them was pungent in her imagination.

Her job ended too soon, and the little garden was planted. Nathan still slept, so Missie sat down beside him on the blanket and listened to the soft gurgle of the spring only a few paces away. It was so good to feel alive again. She thanked God that life was not always winter, that spring always came at last—to chase away the cold and heaviness, and to release one to warmth and movement again.

Nathan awoke and Missie reached for him. She talked to him, encouraging him to behold and enjoy what she saw, to feel the things that she felt, to breathe as deeply as she breathed. But all the baby seemed aware of was the face and arms of the mother who held him close and cooed words of love to him. At length Missie gathered everything together, bundled up her baby, and headed back to her sod house. Nathan was hungry, she knew, and would soon be demanding his own dinner. She would nurse him before preparing their noon meal.

That very night it snowed. When Missie looked out the next morning, hoping to see another fair and sunny day, she saw instead a thin layer of white over the entire world. Willie saw her face and heard her sharp gasp. He joined her at the window, ducking his head so he could look out.

"Moisture!" he said quickly. "Be mighty good fer those

seeds of yers. Soon's the sun's up to work on it, it'll soak in real good."

Missie changed her mind about crying and gave Willie a rueful smile instead. She didn't know if Willie was right, but she wanted him to know that she loved him for his concern for her and her disappointment.

The sun did melt the snow, almost as soon as its warm fingers began to reach out over the brown earth, sending up to heaven little shimmering mists, like dancing vapors.

There were other mornings when Missie awoke to scattered snow or frost on the ground. On such mornings she prayed that none of her brave little plants had as yet lifted their heads from the protective soil bed. Though Missie knew her seedlings were safe as long as they were not exposed, she still longed for their appearance. Daily she watched for signs of life in her garden. Eventually it came—a green blade here and there, a suggestion of a green spray down a row, a pair of tiny leaves breaking forth, gradually joined by others until a row could be defined. At length Missie was able to recognize onions, radishes, beans, peas, and carrots. Her garden was growing.

And then one night—the dreaded frost. Some of the hardier vegetables were seemingly untouched, but the more tender things wilted and curled up tightly against the ground.

"Still plenty of time fer replantin'," Willie assured her. "Ya want me to turn those rows with the spade?"

Missie shook her head. "The exercise will be good for me—and I know how busy you are."

She replanted and again watched for new growth. It came—but it seemed oh so slow this time.

One day as Missie checked on her garden, she was surprised to find an onion plant that looked as if it might be close to being ready. It wasn't that big, really, but when she pulled it up, it truly did smell like an onion. She pulled off its outer skin and popped it into her mouth. Oh, it tasted good! She had almost forgotten how good an onion tasted. Or anything *fresh,* for that matter. She reached for another and devoured it, too. Down the row she went, searching, pulling, and eating, until at length she turned and looked at the trail of discarded tops she had left behind. She was shocked at how many she had eaten. As she bent to pick up the top nearest to her, she felt the results of a lunch of onions. Missie burped—then giggled. "Oh my," she said to herself. "If Willie could see what a pig I've been!"

Guiltily Missie retraced her steps, picking up onion tops so that her gluttony would not be so obvious. She pulled a few more onions to season a stew, then, gathering Nathan up, returned to the house.

The onions did not sit well, and Missie felt an uneasiness in her stomach for the remainder of the day. By the time Willie came for his supper, she wished she didn't have to join him at the table. Even the savory smell of the onions in the stew could not tempt her.

Willie must have observed her white face and instantly showed concern. "Ya sick?"

"Just off my food a little."

"Yer sure?"

"Yeah—I'm sure."

"Ya'd best lie down—I'll look after myself." He led her to their bed. "Where's the problem? Ya got a pain somewhere?"

"Just a little."

"Where?"

"My stomach's a mite upset."

"Taken any of yer ma's medicine? There's stuff there fer—"

"It'll pass."

Willie looked unconvinced. Missie was beginning to *feel* unconvinced, as well. She lay down on the bed, almost groaning as she did so. Willie covered her gently. Then he lifted the box of medical supplies onto the table, sorting through bottles and tins, carefully reading each label.

"Describe what yer feelin'," he said, "an' I'll know better what to look fer."

Missie answered with a loud belch and then a helpless giggle. Willie wheeled around, probably wondering if the loneliness of the western prairies had finally gotten to her, or if maybe she had somehow gotten into some of Cookie's "painkiller." Missie couldn't help herself—she was laughing, not hysterical laughter but controlled mirth.

"I doubt if you'll be finding anything," she said between embarrassed chuckles, "to counteract onions!"

"Onions?"

"*My* onions. They're big enough to eat . . . and I just went right at them and made a pig of myself." She finished her confession with a weak grin.

"Oh, Willie, they tasted so good . . . at first. But," she added seriously, "they're getting so they don't taste nearly so good now."

"Ya mean . . . ya ate onions until. . . ?" Willie asked incredulously.

Missie nodded—and burped again.

The concern was now gone from Willie's face. He lowered himself onto a stool and howled with his own laughter. "Ya little goose," he finally said when he could speak, and they laughed together. He came over to her bed, reached down to kiss her, then backed away.

"Ma'am, you *did* eat onions," he said, wrinkling his nose.

"Put away the medicines. I'll be fine in the morning."

Willie still insisted that she take something for indigestion, then tucked Missie in so she could sleep.

Missie *was* fine again the next morning—but poor Baby Nathan was not. He fussed and fretted all day. Missie scolded herself over and over for not considering him before she attacked the onion patch. But when Missie's stomach had remedied itself and Baby Nathan again slept quietly, Missie smiled to herself. Every mouthful of the fresh, crisp onions had been worth it. They had tasted *that good*—like spring itself.

TWENTY

Summer

Summer was well established, and Missie's garden was daily supplying their table with a variety of tasty fresh produce. Willie had purchased cattle to bolster his herd, and he had decided that his next task would be to hire more riders before the cattle were brought to the Hanging W. This would insure proper protection day and night, once they were wearing his brand. He and Henry spent several days constructing another sod bunkhouse so the hired men would have a place to bed down. After the new dwelling was completed, Willie prepared for a trip to Tettsford Junction to pick up the necessary supplies and also scout out some new ranch hands. He and Henry would each drive a wagon. They left on a Thursday.

Missie looked at her homemade calendar and mentally prepared herself for Willie's three weeks' absence. Oh, how she wished she could have gone, too. She longed so much for a chat with a woman, for a browse through a shop, for tea and cake. But she knew the journey would be long and the weather hot, so she had forced herself to keep from asking Willie if she could go, too. Even if she could have borne the discomfort, she didn't think Nathan would do too well on such a trip.

She wrote notes for Willie to deliver—to Melinda, Kathy, and the preacher and his wife. She then wrote a longer letter to Mrs. Taylorson, bringing her up-to-date on all the things

Nathan could now do—or was attempting to do.

She and Willie worked carefully on the supply list. Missie tried to think of all the things she might need over the next year. And could afford.

It was difficult for Missie to predict everything her growing child would need. Nathan had developed and changed so much already that it was hard to keep up with him even day by day. How could she possibly know what Nathan would need in a year's time? He would be walking and playing outside—needing shoes and shirts and pants. How did one shop for the needs of a fast-growing son? Missie decided that Willie would need some help. She composed a separate list that Willie was to give to Melinda. It was for yarns, sewing fabrics, and two special gifts for Willie—one for his fast-approaching birthday and one for Christmas. She also asked Melinda to choose a small toy for Nathan's first birthday.

Willie tucked away Missie's list for Melinda, then checked and rechecked their supply sheet. He finally turned to Missie.

"Is there anythin' *special* thet ya be wantin'?"

Missie did not hesitate. "Some chickens," she said. "About a dozen hens and a couple of roosters."

Willie's mouth dropped open. "Chickens?"

"Yeah, chickens. Do you realize what it would mean for us to have chickens? We could have eggs—fried, boiled, and scrambled—and roast chicken, fried chicken, chicken and dumplings—"

"Whoa," Willie said. "I'm not doubtin' none the merits of chickens—but *here*?"

"And why not?"

"We don't have the feed."

"They can scrounge for themselves."

"They'd starve!"

"Then we'll just have to buy feed."

"An' they'd need a hen house."

"They could live in a sod hut just as well as I can," said Missie, lifting her chin stubbornly.

Willie must have seen that her mind was made up. "Okay," he laughed. "I'll see what I can do 'bout chickens—but I won't make any promises."

"That's all I'm askin'," Missie said, satisfied that Willie would indeed try.

If Missie had been bored and lonely before, she was doubly so now with Willie gone. Each day she took Nathan out for a short walk or horseback ride. She did not dare go far and could only go out in the morning before the sun got too hot. While Nathan slept she often went to the spring or to her garden. She was pleased her garden was doing well. Each time she went down there she took the time to pull some weeds and pour water on her thirsty plants.

Once in a while she stopped to chat briefly with Cookie. With Willie gone, he seemed to feel responsible for her. Missie was touched by his trips to the spring on her behalf, hobbling along with her buckets of water.

She was careful to stay inside her small hut during the heat of the day and was often surprised that the cozy little soddy of the winter was also cool in the summer. It got awfully still, though, and Missie often yearned for a fresh, cooling breath of summer air, such as she had enjoyed beneath the tall shade trees back home.

The days managed to progress forward, one by one. Soon Missie was down to day eighteen. Her eyes kept searching the distant hills. She hoped that by some miracle Willie would complete his tasks in less time than anticipated and be home early.

One afternoon as Missie's eyes again swept over the hills visible through her window, she was surprised to see a lone rider heading directly toward the house.

Who could that be? she puzzled. *It's sure not Clem or Sandy.* As the rider neared the house, Missie couldn't hold back a gasp of unbelief.

"It's a woman!" she exclaimed aloud, bursting through the door and unexpectedly waking small Nathan with her sharp cry and rush of activity. Tears filled Missie's eyes as she ran toward the rider. She hadn't realized just how starved she was for the company of a woman. Oh, to talk, to laugh, to visit, to sip tea—oh, the joy of it!

Missie brushed away the tears and forced herself to a walk as the woman dismounted—the visitor might be frightened away, thinking she was crazy. They stood and gazed at each other, a smile spreading over their faces. Missie wondered if she detected loneliness in the woman's eyes.

Missie's visitor was hardly more than a girl, with dusky skin, long, loose-flowing dark hair, and black eyes. Her full lips suggested that they liked to laugh. Missie felt drawn to her new friend immediately.

"Oh," she cried, "I'm so glad to see you." She moved forward and threw her arms around the girl, laughing and crying at the same time. The stranger responded, and Missie received a warm hug in return.

They stepped back and studied each other.

"Where did you come from?" Missie asked. To her amazement the girl answered with words she could not comprehend.

Missie frowned.

"I'm sorry," she said, "I don't understand you. You'll have to speak English."

A smooth flow of words followed, but again they meant nothing to Missie.

"You mean, you don't speak English?"

The girl just shrugged. Missie wanted to cry but checked herself and took the girl's arm.

"Well, come in anyway," she said. "At least we can have some tea."

She led the young woman to her tiny sod house and pointed to a stool. She then began to build a fire in her little stove for tea. Upon hearing an exclamation of joy, Missie turned to see the girl bending over Nathan. He had gotten over his fright with Missie's startled exclamation and was lying on the bed playing with his fingers. She looked back at Missie and spoke. From the look in her eyes, Missie took the question to be concerning Nathan and she nodded her head in approval.

The young woman gathered the baby to her, her face full of pleasure. She crooned to him and spoke softly. Nathan could not have understood the words, but he seemed to grasp the meaning, smiling and cooing in return.

The fire caught quickly, and Missie pushed the kettle to the center, then joined the girl.

"Nathan," she said, indicating the baby.

"Na-tan," the girl repeated.

Missie pointed to herself.

"Missie," she said.

"Mis-see." The girl smiled, then added, "Maria," pointing to herself.

"Maria."

There was so much Missie wanted to talk about, so much she wanted to ask. But all they could do was play with Nathan, smile at each other, and sip tea.

At last Maria indicated that she must go. Missie could hardly bear the thought of losing her. She needed her so much—the friendship of another woman. It made her think of her home, of her mother—and the thoughts of her mama made her think of all the precious times they had shared together.

"Wait," she said, "before you go, would it be all right for us to . . . to pray together?"

Maria shrugged, obviously not comprehending.

"Pray," Missie said, pointing to herself and to Maria and then folding her hands for prayer.

"Sí," said Maria, her face lighting up. "Sí." She knelt down beside her stool on the hard-packed earth of the soddy floor. Missie, too, knelt down.

"Dear God," Missie began, "thank you so much for sending Maria to me. Thank you that even though I can't talk with her, I can feel a friendship and warmth. May she be able to come again—soon—and may I be able to learn some of her words so that I can tell her how glad I am to have her. Thank you that we can pray together, and bless her now as she goes home— wherever home is for her. Amen."

Missie prepared to rise, but Maria's soft voice stopped her. Missie opened her eyes and saw her new friend with face upturned in prayer. Her folded hands grasped the beads that hung from her neck.

Maria's voice rose and fell, much like the gentle waters of the creek that ran by Missie's old home. Missie caught "Mis-see" and "Na-tan" in the flow of words and also recognized the "amen."

They rose together and smiled at each other. Missie's cheeks were wet. She had never shared prayer with someone of another language before, of another faith tradition. She only knew that this young woman, Maria, seemed to know Missie's God, and that by sharing these moments together in prayer, their spirits were uplifted and refreshed. Surely God himself had sent Maria. Missie stepped forward and gave her another warm embrace.

TWENTY-ONE

Willie's Return

Missie had struck off the twenty-first day of Willie's trip on her calendar, but still he had not come. There was no sight of dust or wagon on the northern hills, no sound of grinding wagon wheels. She kept his supper hot on the back of the stove, but the fresh biscuits cooled in spite of her efforts. She lit the lamp and tried to read. Her thoughts returned to the verse she had for so many months been clinging to with all her might. She turned in the Bible to read it again. She would not have had to look it up—she knew it by heart. But right then she needed the assurance she could find on the printed page. *Fear thou not; for I am with thee: be not dismayed; for I am thy God: I will strengthen thee; yea, I will help thee; yea, I will uphold thee with the right hand of my righteousness.*

Missie read the verse several times. Eventually she felt quiet enough in her spirit to blow out the lamp and go to bed.

As soon as she got out of bed the next day, she searched the distant hills for small dots that might mean riders, or small clouds that could mean dust from churning wheels and tramping hoofs. But only the glare of the rising sun met her anxious eyes. When dusk came, she was once more forced to give up her vigil. Again that night she read by lamplight and embraced the words of Isaiah 41:10. At length she crawled into bed beside her small son, softly repeating the words to herself in an effort to drive the disquiet from her heart.

The third day dawned, and Missie paced back and forth, scanning the hills for anything that moved. She prepared a third supper for an absent husband and tried to push away the uneasiness within her. *What if Willie doesn't come back?* The question finally demanded her attention, and her thoughts once more went to her mother and the ordeal she had faced when her Clem did not return.

Who was she to think such a thing could not happen to her? Her heart seemed to flutter and then stand still, flutter again and remain silent. Missie threw herself on the bed.

"Oh, God," she wept as she spoke the words aloud, "you know I've been reading and clinging to your Word, but I guess I haven't been believing it, God . . . not really, not down deep in my heart. Help me, Lord. Help me to believe it, to really believe, that no matter . . . no matter what happens, it's in your hands and for my *good*. God, I turn it all over to you . . . my life . . . my Willie . . . everything, dear Father. Help me to trust you with all that is mine."

Missie continued to sob softly until finally a deep sense of peace stole into her heart and gently stilled its wild beating.

She awakened much later to the thumping of hooves in the yard. She pulled herself up quickly and rushed to the window, expecting to see Willie's wagons. Instead, it was several strange horsemen milling about in the bright moonlight. Cookie was approaching them.

"It's happened," Missie whispered, her heart feeling as though it were being squeezed. "Something's happened to Willie." Her weak knees buckled beneath her and she sank onto a stool. "Oh, God, help me now . . . help me to trust you."

She laid her head on her arms on the table and steeled herself for the news that Cookie would bring. No tears came—only a dull, empty feeling.

It was Cookie's footsteps at her door. He called softly and she just as softly bid him enter. He stepped inside, with the moonlight washing over him. Missie knew he could not see her where she sat in the darkness.

"Mrs. LaHaye?"

"Yes."

"Jest thought ya might hear and wonder 'bout all the ruckus in the yard. The new hands thet yer husband hired have jest arrived. The wagons will be in tomorra."

Missie's pounding heart caught in her throat. The new hands! The wagons were a short distance behind them! Willie would be home tomorrow!

It took a moment for it all to sink in. She wanted to shout. She wanted to laugh. She wanted to throw herself on her bed and cry in pure thankfulness. Instead she said in a choked voice, "Thank you, Cookie. I *was* wondering."

When the door was closed and Cookie was gone, she put her head back down on her arms and sobbed out her pent-up feelings in great bursts of joy. "Thank you, God, thank you. Oh, thank you."

———

Missie never told Willie of her anxious days of waiting or of her traumatic nighttime experience. She was sure he would not understand. When the wagons pulled into the yard in the heat and the dust the following day, a calm and smiling Missie greeted her man. He had brought supplies, letters, news that could hardly keep.

Willie turned from Missie to give orders to the ranch hands, then followed her into their small house.

He held her close. "Oh, I've missed ya. I thought thet trail would *never* end. It jest seemed forever." He kissed her. "Did ya miss me—a little bit?" he teased.

"A little bit," Missie said, smiling to herself. "Yeah, a *little* bit," she repeated and returned his kiss.

Willie produced the letters, but even before Missie could read them, Willie had some news.

The preacher's wife had fallen and was laid up with a broken hip. Missie's heart went out to the poor woman.

Kathy Weiss had found herself a young man.

"Poor Henry!" cried Missie.

Willie smiled. "Poor Henry, nothin'. Do ya know, thet young rascal Henry had us all fooled? He wasn't ever after Kathy—not a'tall. It was Melinda Emory, the young widow, right from the start. Only Henry had to wait fer a proper length of time before lettin' her know his feelin's."

"You're not fooling!" Missie spoke incredulously. "Melinda? Well, I'll be!"

"And," Willie went on, "Henry has gone so far as to get some land of his own right next to ours—and in a short while, we'll have neighbors."

Missie could hardly contain herself for joy. Melinda for a neighbor! Another woman she could see often and enjoy her company. She could scarcely wait.

But Willie also had some other big news. "And guess what? They're gonna build a railroad. An' they have it figured to put the main cattle-shippin' station jest eighteen or twenty miles southwest of us . . . maybe even a little closer . . . who knows fer sure? Ya know what thet means? A railroad, a town, people movin' in, connection with the East . . . before we know it, we'll have so many neighbors we'll be trippin' over each other."

Missie exclaimed, "Oh . . . oh," over and over, while amazement and happiness filled her eyes with tears. "Willie, when? When?"

Willie spoke calmly. "Well, I'm sure it won't be tomorra like. But they're workin' on the railroad fer sure . . . from the other end. It should git here within a couple years . . . maybe even next year, some say. An' as soon as the line is in, the people will follow for certain. Always happens thet way. Jest think! A railroad an' shipping station. What thet will mean to the ranchers! No more long cattle drives with heavy losses. Every beef thet gits safely to market means a lot of dollars in a cattleman's pocket." He picked her up and swung her around the room while Nathan watched from his bed, hoping to get in on the excitement, whatever it was.

"We've come at jest the right time, Missie," he said, putting her down after bumping into the table and bed. "Things have never looked better. From now on, every available parcel of land will be snapped up at a big price, an' the price of cattle is bound to go up, too.

"Silly little soddy," he said. "We're gonna git us thet house just as soon as we sell some of the herd next spring. Place ain't fit to live in."

"Oh, Willie," Missie chided—though secretly and silently she agreed with Willie's statement—"it's a home. We can eat, sleep, and keep dry here. That's not bad for starters."

Willie laughed as he hugged her, then went over to swing Nathan up in his arms. "How's the boy?"

"He's been good."

"No more onions?"

"Only a little now and then to flavor a meal."

Willie gazed at his son in his arms. "Look at 'im," he said softly. "He's gone an' growed by inches."

Willie cuddled him close and kissed the soft head of hair while Nathan squirmed. Missie blinked away happy tears.

"Got somethin' fer ya, boy," Willie said to his son. "An' it weren't near the trouble of yer mama's confounded chickens."

"My chickens!" Missie squealed. "Where are they?"

"Well, I hope by now the boys have 'em corralled inside thet wire fence. What a squawkin', complainin' lot they turned out to be!"

"How many?" Missie could barely control her excitement.

"Couple roosters an' eleven hens—an' I had me one awful time to gather up thet many. Folks out here seem to know better than to bother with chickens."

Missie accepted the teasing and hurried out to see her flock. Willie followed behind her with Nathan.

The men had just finished tacking up the wire mesh to poles they had pounded into the ground. As Henry finished hanging the gate that had quickly been built for the enclosure, the other two men turned and left shrugging their shoulders. Let someone else do the fussing with the blamed chickens— they had done more than their share in building the pen.

Willie passed Nathan to Missie and went to lift down the large crate. The chickens squawked and flapped as they were released, not appearing the least bit grateful to be set free. They were a sorry-looking lot, not at all like Marty's proud-strutting chickens back home. Missie wondered if she would ever be able to coax them to produce eggs for her family. One of the hens did not leave the crate. She had succumbed to the heat of the trail or the lice that inflicted her or perhaps some other malady. Willie said he would bury it later so it wouldn't draw any flies.

"Seems to me," he observed, "another good dose of louse powder might not hurt 'em any. I think we'll jest leave 'em outside—shut 'em out of their coop until I treat 'em again. I gave 'em all one good dustin' 'fore I loaded 'em. Left a trail of dead lice from Tettsford Junction to home."

Missie laughed but agreed. They did look like they could stand another good treatment of *something*.

"I'll do the dustin'," Willie said, "but from then on, they're all yers. Never was overfond of chickens, I must say."

Poor Willie. To bring the chickens had been a real ordeal, Missie realized. She looked at him and love filled her heart. Before she could stop herself, the feeling burst forth into words. "Willie," she said, "I love you . . . so much."

Willie dropped a chicken and turned to her, his expression full of his own feelings. "In thet case, Mrs. LaHaye, yer welcome to yer chickens."

Willie's surprise for his young son was a smart-looking half-grown pup. Nathan seemed to instinctively know it was for him, and his chubby hands reached for the fur while the dog licked his face.

"He'll be a big fella when he's full-grown, an' I thought him a good idea," Willie said as he held Nathan in a standing position by the dog. "He'll help to keep the coyotes away from yer chickens. An' ya never know," he said with a grin, "with thet railroad comin an' all those folks pourin' in, ya never know jest who might come callin'. I'd feel safer iffen ya had a good watchdog." He let Nathan sit down beside the puppy and stood to his feet.

Missie looked at the empty miles stretching before her and smiled at Willie's prediction of the crowded countryside. Suddenly she remembered she had not told Willie about her own news.

"Willie, I had a visitor—honest! A real live *woman*—though sometimes I feel I must have dreamed it. Oh, I wish she'd come back. We had the best visit, and we prayed together—"

"Where was she from?"

"I don't know."

"Ya didn't ask?"

Missie laughed. "I asked her lots of things that she didn't

answer—or maybe *did* answer—I don't know . . . and then we just gave up and enjoyed each other."

Willie looked perplexed.

"She couldn't understand English . . . an' I couldn't understand whatever it was that she spoke," Missie tried to explain.

"Yet ya had ya a good visit?"

"Oh yes."

"And ya prayed together?"

Missie nodded in agreement.

"But ya couldn't understand a word the other spoke?"

"Not the words . . . but we could understand the *meaning*. She was really nice, Willie. And young, too. And, oh, I wish so often that she'd come back . . . that we could have tea, and play with Nathan, and laugh and pray together again."

Willie put a hand under her chin and gently lifted her face until he could look into her eyes.

"I didn't know ya were so lonesome," he said huskily. "Here I've been so busy an' so taken up with the spread an' the cows an' all. I never noticed or gave thought to jest how lonesome it'd be fer a woman all alone, without another female nowhere near.

"I shoulda taken ya into town with me, Missie. Given ya a chance to see the outside world again, to visit an' chat. I missed yer need, Missie, an' . . . an' ya never complain . . . jest let me go on makin' dumb mistakes right an' left. A sorry-looking bunch of cowpokes, a work-crazy husband, an' a baby who can't say more than 'goo' ain't much fer company. Yet ya never, never say a thing 'bout it. I love you, too, Missie . . . so very much." They stood for a long moment, arms entwined, until Nathan started to crawl through the dirt after his new playmate.

TWENTY-TWO

Afternoon Tea

While Nathan slept Missie left the house early the next morning to fetch water from the spring for her chickens. She was determined to have eggs for the breakfast table as soon as possible. Already it felt as if it would be a hot day, and she thought of the staleness of the air in their small house on such a day. Perhaps she should take Nathan to the shade bushes near the spring for the most oppressive part of the early afternoon.

She felt lighthearted and hummed as she walked, swinging the empty pail to and fro. Willie was home, she had heard news from dear friends, her strange new world was being enhanced—first with fresh milk, then with her bountiful garden, and now with chickens. It would soon be easy to prepare good meals. She and her family would be able to enjoy many of the things they had been accustomed to back east.

As Missie walked she reviewed parts of the letters she had received. She again felt a pang of sympathy for the misfortune of the preacher's wife. And Mrs. Taylorson! What a kind friend she had turned out to be. She had even sent a pair of tiny shoes to Nathan for when he began to walk—which wouldn't be long at the rate he was growing. Kathy's letter had been full of news of her young man. Seemed he was Samson, Solomon, and the apostle John all rolled into one. Missie smiled. But the letter she had read and reread was the one from Melinda. Knowing that Melinda would one day—*soon,* she hoped—be near enough to be called a neighbor, was very special for Missie. Oh, how she wished Melinda were already here. Another winter in the soddy would be far more bearable with such a friend nearby.

Melinda had written much about the town of Tettsford and her activities with the school and the church. She described the lessening of her pain since the death of her husband, even though his memory still brought tears oftentimes. She also spoke of Henry, of his thoughtfulness, his manliness, and his faith.

Yes, Missie thought, *Henry truly is worthy of a woman like Melinda. They will make such delightful neighbors.*

Missie returned from the spring with the water for her chickens. She talked to them as she poured it into the trough and then portioned out the feed.

"And you better start laying very quickly," she threatened, "or you might find yourselves smothered in dumplings." The chickens fought for rights at the watering trough, paying no mind to Missie's speech.

"You're a motley-looking bunch," Missie said, laughing as she looked at the rather skinny, droopy birds, "but just you wait a week or two. We'll get some meat on those bones and get those feathers smoothed out and back where they belong. Right now you look like you're wearing half of them upside down."

She picked up her pail to hurry back to the house before Nathan would awaken and miss her.

As she rounded the corner of the cook shack, she found Willie and his new hands gathered for a get-acquainted session. The men lounged around in various positions. Some leaned against the sod walls; others squatted on the ground or lay propped up on an elbow. Apparently Willie had let the men know this was a time for "at ease." Cookie sat on his bench near his cook-shack door and was the first to notice Missie. Missie paused a moment to listen.

". . . an' as we'll all be livin' an' workin' together," Willie was saying, "I hope we'll feel free an' easy with one another. By now I'm sure you've all met Scottie, our foreman. Scottie knows all thet there is to know 'bout ranchin'. He'll be takin' over the matters connected with the herd. You'll take all orders from him, an' he'll be responsible to me. You are his concern, an' any requests or complaints thet ya might have are directed to him. If he can't take care of it, he'll see thet I hear 'bout it. He'll assign the shifts an' the jobs, accordin' as he sees fit. Cookie, here, will feed ya. He'll have yer chow waitin' fer ya 'at the same time each day. There'll always be fresh coffee on, fer those comin' an' goin'—even for those on the night shift."

Willie must have noticed Cookie's grin and turned to see Missie standing hesitantly. His eyes lit up.

"An' now fer the bright spot on this here ranch," he said, holding out his hand to her. "I want ya to meet my wife, Mrs. LaHaye."

Missie stepped forward shyly.

"Missie," Willie said, "here are the new riders. Scottie—the foreman." Missie looked into two very kind blue eyes, a twinkle just barely daring to show itself. Scottie looked as weathered and western as the hills that stood behind him. His bowlegged stance spoke of many years in the saddle. Missie felt confidence in Willie's choice of his second-in-command. Scottie, she felt sure, was one to be trusted.

He nodded slightly in acknowledgment of the introduction, his expression conveying, "If you need me, I'm here."

Missie's brief smile was a silent *Thank you.*

Willie moved on. "This here is Rusty." Missie's eyes

traveled over a freckled face and a mop of unruly red hair. A wide grin greeted her.

He's no more than a kid, Missie thought. Her motherly heart wondered about this boy's mama and if she was somewhere worrying and praying for her son. She offered a warm smile.

"An' Smith," Willie continued. Missie turned to look into fierce black eyes in a sun-darkened face. His nod was barely perceptible, and his gaze dropped quickly to the ground. *I wonder,* Missie thought, *what happened to put all that bitterness into your soul.*

"An' Brady," Willie said. Missie looked into another pair of eyes. These were cold and calculating. They seemed too bold and even cruel, making her blush beneath the stare. She nodded quickly, then gave Willie an imploring glance to move on. She could still feel those unnerving eyes upon her.

"An' over here," Willie said, turning to the man who had risen from the ground to acknowledge the introduction, "is Lane."

Lane looked as if he would gladly have willed the earth to open up and swallow him. He started to look at Missie, changed his mind, and looked at the toes of his boots instead, a dark flush spreading steadily over his face. His hands sought something to do or somewhere to go but ended up only rubbing against his sides.

Missie smiled gently, hoping to put him at ease. Never had she seen a man so shy.

Turning from him to the group, she said, "Glad to have you all here at the Hanging W," addressing herself to Scottie in particular. "I know that I won't really be seeing that much of you—you having your work to do and me having mine. But should there ever be a need that my husband and I can help with, we'd be most happy to oblige." She shyly nodded to them all, a small smile crossing her lips. "Now I'd best get back to my baby," she said and turned to the house.

Scottie took over the meeting, and Willie walked to the soddy with Missie.

"Think I found out 'bout yer mysterious neighbor."

"Maria?"

"Yeah."

"How did you find out?"

"Scottie's already been out scoutin' the range. Says they're 'bout seven miles to the south of us. They're Mexican."

"Mexican?"

"Yep. The man speaks some English—but mostly Spanish. Prob'ly had him his own reasons fer strikin' out so far north."

"It couldn't be too serious a reason—it couldn't. I just know Maria would not marry a man who was trying to escape the law or—"

"'Course."

"Maybe they just wanted to be on their own—to make their own way. Lots of people feel that way, all hemmed in by..." Missie decided to let it drop. "And only seven miles?"

"Yep."

"That's not so far, is it, Willie? Just think! Our first neighbors—and so close. Why, I could even ride over and see her— if I knew the way," she finished lamely.

Willie laughed. "Yeah—iffen ya knew the way. An' iffen ya didn't have to ford a river to get there. An' iffen ya knew some Spanish. *Then* ya could make a visit. But I shouldn't joke. I promise I'll do my best to take you over to our new neighbors. In the meantime, why don't ya learn a little Spanish? It would be a real nice surprise for Maria."

"But how can I?"

"Cookie. Cookie knows 'bout everything there is to say in the Spanish tongue. He worked fer a Spanish family when he was little more'n a kid. I got the feelin' when I heard him talk 'bout 'em he kinda wishes thet he'd stayed with 'em—but at the time he was young an' had the wander bug. He's 'bout crossed the whole continent on horseback since, it seems, workin' on spreads as he's traveled."

"Oh," said Missie, alarmed. "I do hope he won't decide to leave us. I—"

"Not much chance of thet. He's not as young as he used to be, nor as adventurous, either. An' I'm thinkin' thet he don't sit a horse near as comfortable since he had his fall."

"And he knows Spanish?"

"He sure does. Mind ya, though," Willie teased some more, "thet he doesn't teach ya *all* the words he knows. Some of 'em ain't very ladylike."

"Do you think he would—*teach* me, I mean?"

"I'm sure he'd be glad for an excuse to git off his bad leg occasionally."

―――

So Missie timidly approached Cookie about the possibility of Spanish lessons. He was delighted to help out, and they began with their first lesson down by the spring that very day. She had only advanced as far as *buenos días* and *adiós* when Maria arrived again.

Maria cuddled Nathan, all the time directing a steady stream of flowing Spanish, first to the baby and then to Missie. When Missie smiled and nodded, Maria's Spanish flowed even more rapidly. At length Missie could bear it no longer.

"Wait," she said to Maria, gesturing with her hands. "Don't go away—I'll be right back. You just sit right down and hug my baby. I'm going to get us both some help."

Missie hurried out the door, realizing as she ran to the cook shack that Maria, like herself, had not understood one word of the exchange.

"Cookie," Missie panted out, her voice pleading, "would you mind, please . . . please, would you have tea . . . with two ladies?"

Cookie's eyes grew round with dismay.

"Oh, please," Missie begged. "Maria has come again, and I can't understand her Spanish—not one word except 'buenos días.' And she can't understand me. And we're just dying to say something to each other. Please, could you just this once . . . please? I'll make you coffee if you prefer," Missie quickly promised.

Cookie's good-natured face crinkled into a begrudging smile. He wiped his hands on his greasy apron, which he removed and cast aside.

"Iffen it means thet much," he agreed.

"Oh, it does, it does."

"Fer a few minutes," Cookie amended. "Gotta git back to the steak I'm poundin'. But I can spare a few minutes. An' I reckon I can pass up the coffee an' drink yer tea—long as it ain't in one a' them fancy little cups."

Missie hurried with him to the sod house.

"Maria," she called triumphantly as they approached. "Here's Cookie! He knows Spanish!" When Cookie turned to Maria with a fluent welcome in her own tongue, Maria clasped her hands with a merry laugh, and silvery-sounding Spanish arced between them.

Cookie turned to Missie and shrugged. "She says this is gonna be more fun than a fiesta," he said, but the look in his own eyes still indicated doubt. Missie poured his tea into a big mug and passed him some fresh bread and butter.

Cookie fell into the spirit of the visit and soon seemed to be enjoying his time at the tea party almost as much as the two young women. Missie was careful to keep his mug of tea replenished and to make sure the bread was within his reach.

He didn't seem to mind even their female talk, which he had to translate back and forth.

When Maria prepared to go, the two truly did feel like *neighbors*. Missie gave her promise, through Cookie, that Willie would bring her over sometime soon.

"Cookie *también?*" Maria teased, and Missie needed no translation. They both laughed as Cookie muttered and grinned.

"I know you're busy, Cookie," Missie said as he bounced little Nathan on his knee, "and I thank you so much for taking the time. It's all right. We'll let you go now."

Cookie put Nathan down and declared he had to get back to supper fixings. But Missie noticed he took his time about leaving.

"Muchas gracias," Maria added her thanks, and Cookie shuffled off to return to his cook shack.

Maria's next comment came with actions rather than words, and Missie enthusiastically nodded her agreement to pray together.

Again the two young women—of different races, different cultures, different religious backgrounds—knelt together in the small kitchen and poured out their hearts to the one true God who could hear in any language. Missie could tell that Maria's need and longing for fellowship in the faith was as real and deep as her own.

Missie prayed, "Please, dear God, may I quickly learn enough of Maria's Spanish to be able to share with her about matters of faith, about the life I have received through the death and life of your Son. I long so much to talk about you, your love and forgiveness, and to study the Bible together. Help me, God, to learn Spanish soon." Missie added one more thought, "And dear God, help Cookie to know the right words to teach me."

TWENTY-THREE

Another Winter Ahead

Missie and Willie made plans for the promised trip to their new neighbors, Maria and Juan, two weeks after Maria's last visit. Missie tried to cajole Cookie into accompanying them, but Scottie, who could also speak a little Spanish, went with them instead. When the day came for the trip, Missie felt far more inclined to ride her horse than travel in a bumpy wagon. Little Nathan was lifted up to share his father's saddle, and the four started off, Scottie setting a leisurely pace in spite of Missie's impatience to reach their destination.

The fording of the river gave Missie some inner butterflies, and she saw again in her mind's eye the Emorys' bobbing, tilting wagon and the plunging terror-stricken horses. But once her horse was in and swimming strongly, Missie realized the current was not that swift.

They found Juan and Maria in a sprawling stone house that was cool and comfortable. Missie decided right away that she would prefer stone to any other available material. Juan was pleased to show Willie around and explain the process of building such a home. It wasn't the style of house Missie had been used to, but it was cool against the heat of the day and seemed so spacious after their small soddy. Juan promised his help when the day arrived for Willie to begin the building.

The four took their leave well before dark. Mountain rains

had swollen the river waters, and Scottie declared them to be higher than normal for the time of year. And even though it was not considered dangerous, he wanted to ford the river in full daylight.

Maria and Missie told each other there was great comfort in knowing another woman lived within visiting distance.

When they reached home, Willie took Missie's horse and passed Nathan to her. Missie lingered outside, enjoying the cool of the late afternoon.

Willie turned and called back to her, "Hold supper a bit, will ya? I'm gonna ride on up to the upper spring an' see iffen it's still flowin' enough fer the cattle over thet way. I should be back in an hour or two."

Missie agreed, glad for the extra time before lighting the fire in the stove. She placed Nathan on the ground, guiding his tottering steps toward their small home. How shabby and tiny it looked compared to Maria's. Missie would be so thankful to have more room, a floor for rugs, and windows big enough from which to hang curtains. She heard Willie's horse leave the yard as she laid Nathan down for a much-needed nap. He was sound asleep before Missie had completed a row on the sock she was knitting.

She looked up in surprise at a knock on the door. Maybe Henry had found time for a chat. She hadn't seen him since their Sunday "church" time. She stepped to the door and opened it, fully expecting Henry—or Cookie. But it was Brady. Missie fidgeted beneath the smile he tried on her and the intensity of his eyes.

"Oh . . ." she began, but he moved past her and entered the room. Missie felt the air tighten around her.

" 'Scuse me fer intrudin', ma'am," he said, but there was no apology in his voice. "I thought maybe you bein' a woman thet ya could help me out some."

Missie remembered her lightly spoken promise of help if there was a need. A strange fluttery feeling made her wish she hadn't been so quick to speak. She did not move from the door.

"I seem to have picked up a sliver in my finger here, an' do ya know, there's not one of those mangy ol' cowpokes thet has 'em a needle."

"Oh," Missie said again, and then life returned to her limbs. "Oh yes . . . I have needles. Of course." Missie moved from the open door to her sewing basket and heard the door close behind her.

She fumbled with a package of needles and finally disengaged one she thought was the proper size. As she rummaged, her mind whirled. *What is Brady doing here? At this hour of the day all hands are normally busy checking cattle, mending fences, fixing gear—something. I haven't even noticed Cookie about—oh yes, I did. As we rode up, Cookie was heading for the spring with two water pails.*

She turned with the needle to find Brady standing close behind her.

"Here you are," she said, trying to keep her voice steady. But he didn't take the needle extended to him.

"I'm afraid, ma'am, thet I'll have to ask you to be kind enough to work thet little bit of a tool fer me. My hands never were any good with anything thet size."

"Me?" Missie asked dumbly, thinking there was no way she was going to bend her head and work over this man's hand as she held it in her own. She could almost feel his breath upon her now in the closeness of the small room.

"I'm sorry," she said evenly. "You'll have to do it yourself— or else ask Cookie to help you."

"Now, ma'am," the cowboy murmured, inching closer. Even in the dimness of the soddy, Missie could see his eyes seem to darken. "Don't tell me yer man-shy?"

He reached a hand out to touch her arm and Missie stepped backward, feeling the side of the bed as she bumped up against it. She wanted to scream, but her throat tightened in a dryness that she had never felt before. She thought her knees were going to give way beneath her. A short but fervent prayer welled up within her. *Oh, God, strengthen me, help me, uphold me as you promised.*

Then the door swung open. "Mrs. LaHaye?" There had been no knock, but there stood Scottie. "The boss home?"

You know he's not, Missie responded to herself. *You heard him say he was going to the upper spring.*

Instead, she said nothing. She shut her eyes to muster enough strength to remain on her feet.

"Brady?" said the foreman as though surprised. "Got those fences checked already?"

Brady twisted around, his face full of anger. Without a word he slammed out through the door. Scottie pulled out a stool for Missie. She accepted it without speaking. Then he walked to the pail and handed her a small dipper of water. She was surprised to find she could still swallow.

"Brady had himself a problem, ma'am?" Scottie asked lightly, but Missie noted that his voice was edged with steel.

"A sliver . . . in his hand."

"You fix it?"

She looked down at the needle she still held in her trembling hand and shook her head. "I told him he'd have to do it himself . . . or get Cookie."

"Did he bother you?"

"No," Missie replied shakily, "no, but something about him frightens me. I only know. . ." She swallowed again. "Here," she said, holding out the needle, "would you give it to him?"

"Thet's all right, ma'am. Keep yer needle. I'll look after Brady." Then he was gone, gently closing the door behind him.

Missie sat for some time before she felt her legs strong enough to stand. At length she was able to stir herself. She went over to lay a trembling hand on her sleeping son and whisper, "Thank you, Lord, for protecting us." She turned to build a fire for preparing Willie's supper.

She said nothing to Willie that night—not yet. But she vowed to keep an eye out for Brady. She'd put some kind of lock on the inside of the door if she had to. There was no way that man would enter her house again.

The next morning as she left the house to go to the spring for water, she glanced about furtively. *How dreadful not to feel safe in one's own yard,* she thought. Then she heard voices coming from the side of the bunkhouse. One was Willie's voice, and with the words came renewed courage for Missie.

"Henry says thet Brady drew his pay."

"Yep," Scottie replied.

"Not happy ridin' fer me?"

"He didn't say nothin' 'bout bein' unhappy."

"But he quit?"

"Nope." And after a pause, "I fired 'im."

"Thought he was known to be *good* with cattle." Willie's voice seemed to suggest a shrug of his shoulders as though he couldn't quite understand the situation, but Scottie was in charge where the cowhands were concerned.

"Reckon he was." Scottie was noncommittal.

"Reckon you had yer reasons," Willie said.

"Yeah," Scottie said softly, "reckon I did."

Missie continued on her way to the spring. Her world suddenly belonged to her again—her garden, her chickens, her house. She could count on Willie's men to care not only for his cattle but to care for her and Nathan, as well. And with Willie's men and her heavenly Father, she really had no need to worry. None at all.

Missie placed a chair in the shade of the sod house and continued her work on a pair of trousers for Nathan. His dog lay nearby, already grown almost to full size. The black mongrel showed some intelligence, and he was ever so gentle with young Nathan. For the gentleness, Missie allowed him her devotion.

It was cool in the evenings now, and Missie was thankful for the relief from the intense summer heat. For many days she had been busy canning the produce from her garden. As she watched it stack up around her, she began to wonder where she would keep it from freezing over the long winter. Unless she could persuade Willie to dig a root cellar, they would have to bury the food in the hay in the barn. Missie wished again for a new bigger house, but she held her tongue. She knew it would be hers as soon as Willie was able.

She looked up from her work and saw Henry approaching. "Hi, stranger," she teased. "I'd begun to wonder if you were still riding for this outfit. I haven't seen you for so long."

"It's this boss I got," Henry responded. "Don't know nothin' but work, work, work!"

Missie laughed.

"But then," Henry added, "guess he can't be all bad. He's promised me two weeks off."

"Really? You're going to make a trip?"

Henry flushed. "I sure am," he offered. "Jest as fast as ol' Flint can carry me. Seems like downright years since I last saw—"

"I'm so happy for you and Melinda," Missie said. "She must be missing you, too, something awful."

"I sure hope so," Henry said. "Iffen she misses me half as much . . ." He let the sentence hang.

"Have you set a date?" Missie asked. "Or am I being nosy?"

"Don't mind yer interest none. An' no, not yet. Sure wish thet we could, but it depends."

"On what?"

"On how soon I can build me a house."

"With a little help, you can have a house up in a few days."

"I mean a *house,* Missie, not a soddy."

Missie was surprised at the intensity of Henry's reply.

"I agree," she said carefully, "that there's not much inviting about a soddy, but it can be a home—be it ever so simple and confining."

"I'd never ask Melinda to live in such conditions—never," Henry said heatedly. "Don't you think thet I saw the look in yer eyes when ya spotted the dirt floor, the dingy windows, the crowded—"

"Henry," Missie interrupted softly but steadily, "answer me honestly. Do you still see that look there now? That look of surprise, of hurt, of disappointment? Is it still there?"

Henry paused to look into her face, then shook his head. "No," he said, "I guess not. You've done well, Missie. Really great . . . an' I've admired ya fer it. A girl like you . . . leavin' what ya had, an' comin' way out here to this. I've truly admired ya. But, beggin' yer pardon . . . I won't ask thet of Melinda."

"An' I respect you for your thoughtfulness concerning her, Henry. But you should know something." Missie stopped to choose her words. "Henry, I want you to know that I'd far sooner share this little one-room dirt dwelling with Willie than to live in the world's fanciest big white house without him. And I mean that, Henry."

Henry chuckled softly, but his expression held wonder.

"You women are strange creatures indeed," he said. "It's a marvel we men ever succeed in understandin' ya a'tall. But I do thank the good Lord fer makin' ya the way ya are." He paused to look again into her face. "Ya really do mean thet, don't ya?"

"I really do," Missie said. And deep in her heart she marveled at just how much she meant it. The glory of that truth somehow unshackled her spirit from the small, shabby little dwelling, to soar far above it in the strength of her love for Willie. Somehow, the long, unwelcome winter ahead did not look so frightening now, even though she still faced being shut away inside the one confining room. She and Willie and Nathan might be crowded together, but they were bundled comfortably in the blanket of love.

TWENTY-FOUR

Sundays

When Henry returned from visiting his Melinda, Missie sensed about him a new depth of loneliness. She wondered if he was silently realizing that perhaps love could have seen them through a winter in a little sod house, but Henry never admitted as much. He missed Melinda—that was very evident. He often found excuses to drop by the soddy and chat or play with Nathan to help fill the lonely hours in between work.

Missie noticed that Henry and the young Rusty seemed to enjoy each other's company and often rode out together. Missie knew Scottie wisely tried to team up the men who worked well together. In the evenings in the bunkhouse, Henry was teaching Rusty to strum his guitar. The two young cowboys spent many hours singing range songs and old hymns.

One Sunday as Willie, Missie, and Henry sat talking after the three of them had their usual time of Bible reading, hymn singing, and prayer, they discussed the coming railroad, the people it would bring, future shops, schools, and even a doctor.

Then Willie said with deep feeling, "Ya know what I long fer most? A church. I jest ache sometimes to gather with a larger group of believers and sing an' pray an' read the Word. And hear a real sermon. It seems like so long . . . what I wouldn't give fer jest one Sunday back home."

Missie felt her eyes become misty. A Sunday back home

meant Pa with his baritone voice expressing his praise, Ma in her quiet, confident manner joining in. It meant Clare and Arnie, Ellie and little Luke gathered around. It meant Nandry and Clae and their families. Missie wondered if there were more members to those families by now, how tall Clare was, if Arnie still teased Ellie, and if everyone outdid each other spoiling little Luke. She wondered if her mother Marty still looked west each night and breathed a prayer for her faraway little girl, and if Pa still lifted down the family Bible and read with a steady, assured voice the promises of God. *Are they all well . . . my family?* If only there was some way to span the miles, as Willie had put it, to spend a Sunday at home.

Missie blinked away her tears and came back to the reality of their small home.

"It would be so good to hear the Word with others," Willie was saying. "I'll be awful glad when we have enough neighbors to have our own little church and a preacher."

Then Willie was looking around the room, seeming to size it up. "Remember how we all managed to crowd in here fer Christmas?"

"Yeah, we were toe to toe—but we fit," Missie laughed.

"Well, we can fit again," Willie said. "Boy, have I been dumb!"

He reached for his hat. "I'm gonna go find the rest of our *congregation,*" and he ducked quickly through the door.

And so it was that all the hands working on the Hanging W Ranch were invited to share Sunday services in the little sod house.

That next Sunday only Rusty came with Henry, but what a time they had singing the old hymns, accompanied by Henry's guitar, and reading the Scriptures together. The next Sunday it was Henry and Rusty again.

A couple of Sundays later, Cookie hobbled in, clearing his

throat and looking a bit embarrassed. He'd been heard to say that "religion was fer the weak and fer women."

In spite of ridicule from the hardened Smith (who, whenever he was asked his full name snapped, "It's Smith—jest Smith," making Missie wonder if he truly had a claim to even that), the weeks passed with attendance gradually growing. By Christmas Sunday, Smith was the only holdout. He saddled his horse and rode away into the quietness of the snow-covered hills. Missie prayed that God might somehow reach his cold, unhappy heart.

After their service together, Missie managed to serve them a special Christmas dinner. She even had been tempted to sacrifice two of her chickens for the occasion but could not bring herself to do so. She was getting four or five eggs a day, and as she still hadn't determined who were the producers and who were the sluggards, she granted them all extended life, lest she slaughter the wrong ones.

With her milk, eggs, and a few hoarded raisins, she made some bread pudding. Even those who did not care for the chickens themselves did not scorn what the hens were able to produce. They smacked their lips in appreciation as they went back for seconds.

Nathan thoroughly enjoyed the whole crowded celebration. He shook his head sadly when the last figure left the small soddy. "Aw gone," he sighed, "Aw gone."

After having taken the plunge for Christmas Sunday, the last of the men who'd been reluctant about "religion" continued to join the regular Sunday services. Unless duty called them away, at the appointed time of two o'clock they all, except for Smith, entered the house, dusting the snow from their coats with their hats and stamping their boots. Then they quietly found places to sit for the short time of singing, Bible reading, and prayer.

Missie prayed for Rusty, the easygoing, openhearted young

boy of the group. He eagerly sang the old hymns and listened attentively as the Scripture was read. She hoped his heart was being touched by the truth.

But it was the shy, backward Lane who knocked on their door one evening and mumbled in an embarrassed voice, "Is the boss in?"

Missie welcomed him in, and he stood facing Willie, nervously twisting his hat in his hand.

"I wondered, boss, iffen y'all wouldn't mind . . . iffen you'd . . ." He cleared his throat. "I don't have much understandin' 'bout the things of the Bible. Could ya . . . would ya sorta go over it again . . . slow like, iffen ya don't mind?"

So Lane was invited to sit down at the table, and by the light of the flickering lamp, with fresh cups of coffee before them, he and Willie again went over the words of the Book while Missie silently prayed.

"'If thou shalt confess with thy mouth the Lord Jesus," read Willie, "'and shalt believe in thine heart that God hath raised him from the dead, thou shalt be saved.'"

Missie was sitting off to the side, her hands finding jobs to do for which she needed little light. She was praying that God would bless His Word and open the understanding of the young man.

Her heart was full. God had been good to Willie and her. And He had given them their own unique, and very special, *congregation*.

Missie's second winter in the soddy was nearing its end.

The winds seemed to be abating, and she even dared to hope for an early thaw. Already she was mentally planning her garden, though she knew full well that it would be weeks before she could actually do the planting. This year, she promised herself, she would listen to Willie and not rush the season. But she wondered if her logic could hold her eagerness in check.

This spring she hoped to have some setting hens, as well. Though she still made use of her daily egg supply, she had been holding some back each day for the sittings. A spring calf was due to Ginger, one of their two milk cows. In no way could Willie's anticipation of the dozens of range calves expected compare to Missie's excitement for that one calf that would be born to the cow in the barn. Pansy was still milked daily, although her supply was running low. It would soon be time for her to take a rest from the daily production and wait for her calf that was yet some months away.

And then there was the promised house to look forward to! Missie had fretted about it, fearing that the money shouldn't be spent on one for an additional year. But Willie was determined that the start be made on their stone home as soon as possible. A good share of the outer material was almost free, he assured her, and the labor would be cheap.

With Scottie to oversee the activities of the ranch, Willie would be free to get on with the building. Juan also had promised him two helpers who had a great deal of experience with stone buildings. Willie sat at night at the small table, and he and Missie talked over plans for the house. The low rambling stone building would be built with the main living area in the middle, the kitchen and dining area located in the left wing and the bedrooms in the right. A shaded porch and small courtyard would provide a good spot for Missie to sit and do handwork while young Nathan enjoyed the out-of-doors. Willie sketched out the plans, then redrew them, over and over. Missie tried to restrain herself, not daring to let the hope become too real lest something happen to prevent it.

But she did her share of dreaming.

Oh, the fun she would have unpacking all their stored things—the proper-sized stove, the sewing machine, the rugs, the curtains, the fancy dishes. At times she thought she would burst in her eagerness.

Henry had decided that with the spring, he also would do some building. He had bought the land bordering Willie's and had plans to put his house just as close to the LaHayes' home as he could, so it would be convenient for the women to visit and do things together. Missie could scarcely wait for Melinda to arrive.

Willie agreed to sell Henry fifty head of cattle, with whatever calves were at heel, so Henry could get a start on his own spread. This would also give Willie some cash for the new house. If Scottie disapproved of a cattleman making sales of stock in the spring, he did not say so. He no doubt knew the transaction would assist both men in realizing their dreams.

Rusty decided to go to work on Henry's spread, so Scottie needed to find two more hands for the Hanging W. He assured Willie he would take his time and choose carefully.

Scottie reported that the outlying ranches were already planning a fall trail drive to move their cattle to the market. If Willie wanted to, he could send as many head of cattle as he wished, along with a designated number of riders. Willie decided he'd hold his herd that year unless unexpected expenses demanded more cash. Everyone was hopeful that before another fall rolled around, the railroad would have made its promised appearance. This would eliminate the costly, time-consuming, wearying trail drive.

This winter's losses seemed to be low, and the calf crop looked good. As each count came in, Missie's hopes for the new home mounted. She anticipated the summer before her, and even the thought of the approaching heat was not able to shrivel her spirits. She gazed across the endless hills. She and

Willie had lived in the area such a short time and already they were seeing changes—and the future promised many more. Would they all come true—the dreams, the plans? Whatever the outcome, things were going well now. She was sure, for the first time, that if they really needed to, they could carry on indefinitely just as they had been living.

She decided that as soon as Nathan woke from his nap, she'd ride up to the top of the hill for a look at the distant mountains. She was wondering what color they would appear on this bright springlike morning.

Cookie appeared at the cook-shack door carrying a dishpan. He tossed the water carelessly to the side of the path and stopped to look up at the sky. Missie wondered if he also was willing spring to come.

TWENTY-FIVE

Nathan

Willie went to check the horses before retiring while Missie finished the dishes and prepared Nathan for bed.

"You are getting so big," she told the little boy. "Soon you aren't going to fit in that wee bed anymore. Your pa is going to have to make you a bigger one."

Nathan smiled, "Big boy."

Missie kissed his chubby cheeks. "Big boy, all right. You are Mama's big boy."

Nathan returned her kiss in his damply affectionate fashion.

"Now," Missie said, "let's say our prayers."

Missie prayed, stopping often to let Nathan try to repeat her words. He finished with a hearty " 'men." As Missie tucked him into bed, she noticed his breathing sounded heavier than usual.

"I do hope you're not coming down with a cold," she told him. "Won't be long now until the days will be nice and sunny and warm, and you can go outside to play as much as you like."

"Doggie?"

"Sure, you can play with your doggie. You always think of 'doggie' when I talk about outside, don't you? Well, soon now you can be out with Max as much as you want to."

Nathan seemed to like the idea.

Missie pulled the blanket up under his chin and kissed him

again, then began to refill the lamp with oil. Willie might wish to work on the house plans again.

Willie returned and, as Missie expected, pulled his stool up to the table. He still wasn't sure the entrance to the house was in the most convenient place. He tried various drawings, first shifting it one way and then the other. Missie watched and made suggestions while she darned a sock. Willie finally decided his first choice had been the right one.

The next day's branding was bound to be long and tiring, and they went to bed early.

Missie lay for a few moments listening to Nathan's breathing, then Willie's snoring drowned out the sound. She felt a tightness in her stomach as she turned over to try to go to sleep but couldn't decide just why.

Missie wasn't sure who awakened first, she or Willie. But she suddenly realized she was sitting upright in bed, a feeling of panic making the blood pound in her ears. Already Willie was springing from the bed.

"What is it?" Missie called in the darkness.

"It's Nathan! He's chokin' somethin' awful."

Missie heard it then—the rattling gasp for breath.

"Oh, dear God, no!" she cried and stumbled out of bed after Willie.

"Light the lamp," Willie ordered, already reaching for the small boy.

Missie hurried to fetch it, her bare feet feeling the coolness of the dirt floor.

"What is it? What's the matter with him, Willie?"

"Was he okay when ya put him to bed?"

"He was a little raspy sounding, but nothing like this. Oh, Lord, what can we do? What is it, Willie?" Missie cried, her heart tearing at each ragged breath of her baby.

No doctor! her mind screamed with each wild beat. No

doctor! Not for miles and miles! No help anywhere near here!

"Have you ever seen this before in any of yer family?" Willie asked frantically.

"Never!" replied Missie, the tears overflowing. "Never! I've no idea what it might be. Unless—could it be pneumonia? He can't breathe." *Oh, dear God, we need you now,* her heart cried. *Little Nathan Isaiah needs you now. Please, dear God, show us what to do, or send us some help—someone who knows. Please, God.*

"Have ya some medicine?" implored Willie. "Some things from yer ma? Where do ya keep it, Missie?"

"All I ever brought in were the first-aid supplies. There's more still stored in the barn, though. I've never unpacked it—never needed it—"

"I'll git it—ya stay and keep 'im warm, Missie."

"No, Willie, you wouldn't know the box—it'll take you too long to find it. I'll go, I know just where it is."

Missie pulled on her boots and shoved her arms into the sleeves of Willie's coat, then quickly lit another lantern. She ran from the house, the mud and slush from the spring puddles splashing on her bare legs.

"Oh, heavenly Father," her prayers continued aloud as she gasped for breath, "please help us. We don't have a doctor. We don't even have a neighbor near. We don't know what to do. Please help us, God. I couldn't bear to lose him. I just couldn't, God." The tears poured down her cheeks.

She found the box of medicines quickly enough and ran with it back to the house, still pleading, "Oh, please, God, please save my baby."

As she neared the soddy she could see inside through the tiny window. Willie stood with the baby in his arms. He was praying. Missie saw his tears and the anguish on his face.

"Oh, dear God," she prayed, coming to a sudden stop. "It's Willie's *son,* his pride and joy, God. If you must take our baby . . . be with my Willie. Give him the strength to bear it, God. He loves his boy so much. Oh, dear God, please help us, please, please help us . . . if only someone knew. . . ." She tried to silence her sobs as she hurried into the house.

She placed the wooden box on the table. Without removing the heavy coat, she frantically clawed at the lid with a hammer from a peg near the door. The lid came loose with a loud squeak. She rummaged through the medicines, having no idea what she should be looking for.

Willie paced the floor, holding young Nathan upright in an effort to ease his troubled breathing. Suddenly there was a "hullo" outside the door, and without even waiting for a reply, Cookie walked in.

He did not ask questions. His eyes and ears must have already taken in the answers because he announced, "Croup!" in a loud voice.

"What?" Willie exclaimed.

"Croup."

"You know what it is?"

"Sure do. Thet breathin'—thet's croup."

"Can you. . . ?" Missie was afraid to ask.

"Can sure try. Git the fire goin'. Make it as hot as ya can and git some water boilin' fast."

Willie handed the struggling baby to Missie and hurried to comply. He filled the stove with cow chips and soaked them with fuel from the lamp. A brisk fire was soon blazing. Willie set the kettle directly over the flame, though it still seemed to take forever to boil.

Cookie placed a stool in the middle of the room.

"Git me a blanket."

Willie whipped a blanket from their bed.

"Now we need a basin fer the water."

Willie pulled the dishpan from its hook.

Cookie busily dug through the medicines Missie had strewn across the table. He carefully read the labels that had been placed on each one by Missie's mother.

"This oughta do," Cookie said. "Got a spoon?"

Willie handed him one and Cookie poured out a large helping of the ointment and dumped it into the basin. The water finally boiling, Cookie poured it into the pan and held out his arms for the baby. Missie was reluctant, but Cookie seemed to be their only hope. She passed over their beloved son.

"Put some more water on and keep thet fire goin'," Cookie ordered and sat down on the stool. "Now push thet basin over here, an' toss thet blanket over the both of us. We gotta have us a good steam bath."

They covered the two and then waited silently. Willie poked at the fire, and Missie paced the floor in the small space left to her, praying and listening painfully to Nathan's choking, rasping efforts to breathe. The minutes ticked by. From beneath the heavy blanket came Cookie's voice, startling both Willie and Missie.

"Thet other water boilin' yet?"

It was.

"Pull out this here basin an' change the water. Put in another spoonful of the medicine, too."

It was done, and Willie pushed the steaming pan back under the blanket tent, being careful not to release the buildup of steam already trapped within.

Again Missie paced and prayed while Willie poked at the fire and prayed. He stuffed in another chip every time he could possibly make one fit. The room was becoming unbearably hot.

Nathan began to fuss. *Was he worse?* Further panic seized Missie.

"Good sign," Cookie called out. "Before, he was too busy

fightin' fer breath to bother to fight the steam. His breathin' seems to be easin' some."

It has, Missie thought with wild joy. *He's not choking nearly as much.* Her tears began to fall as she repeated softly to herself, " 'Fear thou not; for I am with thee: be not dismayed; for I am thy God: I will strengthen thee; yea, I will help thee . . .' " Missie could go no further. Sobs of thankfulness were crowding out all other thoughts. "Oh, dear God, thank you, thank you."

Willie made another change of water, passing it to Cookie beneath the blanket. Nathan stopped fussing and his breathing steadily improved.

"He's asleep now," Cookie announced in a loud whisper. "He seems able ta breathe without too much strugglin'."

Missie's arms ached to hold her baby, but Cookie kept him under the blanket.

The first streaks of dawn were reaching their golden fingers toward the eastern hills before Cookie ventured to lift the blanket from his head.

"Put on the coffeepot, would ya, missus?" was his only comment.

Willie reached to take away the blanket and move the basin.

Missie woodenly filled the coffeepot and put it on the stove. She then turned to Cookie, who was handing the sleeping baby to his father.

"Put him back to bed now," he said, then added slowly, "This might come again fer a night or two, but iffen yer watchin' fer it, ya should be able to ward it off. In a few nights' time he should be over it. Croup always hits like thet—in the dead of night, scarin' one half to death. The steamin' helps."

Missie looked at the little man. He spoke quietly, matter-of-factly, as though he were used to working miracles. His body appeared limp, his clothes soaked with steam and perspiration, his wispy hair clinging wetly against his scalp. His face was drained and white, and glistened with moisture in the early morning light. Yet Missie's heart cried out that he was truly the most beautiful person she had ever seen.

She crossed the room and reached out to gently touch his soft, stubbled face. "Cookie Adams," she said, tears and laughter in her voice, "you can't fool me—not for a minute. You're no grouchy, hard-riding ole cowpoke at all. You're a visiting *angel*."

TWENTY-SIX

Love Finds a Home

Missie finally planted her garden and set her hens. Green things soon appeared and so did soft, fluffy yellow chicks— eighteen of them. Missie rejoiced, thinking ahead to leafy vegetables and fried chicken. Even Willie admitted that her idea of raising chickens was not such a bad one after all. The cow calved, a fine young heifer. Missie's milk supply was assured for many months ahead.

Willie, with the instructions of Juan and his men to guide him, began the work on the house, just a few yards east of the soddy. Day after day Missie watched excitedly as it took shape.

Henry had left for his own nearby ranch. Missie missed him and the redheaded Rusty. She was always glad to welcome them back for a visit or a meal. Henry and Rusty still joined them for their gathering each Sunday, and Missie and Willie were glad to have them. She wasn't sure yet how Willie's two new hands felt about working on a spread where the boss had Sunday singsongs and Bible reading. So far, they had chosen to follow Smith's lead and stay away from such goings-on.

Willie took time from his house building to ride over to Juan's for a meeting of cattlemen. Missie itched to go along, but she knew that chatting women and a business meeting of the men might not mix too well. She contented herself with plans for a visit on some future day, when she and Maria could enjoy each other's company without interruption. Maria's English was improving even faster than Missie's Spanish, and the two young women spent much of their infrequent visits laughing at each other's mistakes and celebrating new levels of communication.

When Willie returned from the meeting, he was bursting with news. A group of men had been in to stake out a site for the train station, he told Missie. Land already was sold for a general store. He was certain that other buildings would soon follow. And the best news was that the station would be only fifteen miles away! An easy trip in one day! No more two-week supply trips to Tettsford Junction. The first train was due to come chugging in during early spring of the following year.

The thought nearly took Missie's breath away. To have supplies come in so close, to be able to make a trip to town, to greet people and walk on sidewalks—it was all too overwhelming to comprehend.

"Sure, it'll take time—but it'll all come," Willie declared. "An' guess what else? Thet there train station is gonna be more'n jest a cattle-shippin' place. It's gonna have a post office, too. We'll be able to mail letters right here an' git answers back from our folks."

Missie caught her breath. Just to be able to write home to her mama and pa! To be able to tell them of Nathan's progress, of her new house, of Cookie—their faithful old ranch hand sent to them by God himself, though Cookie didn't realize that yet—of her chickens, her garden. Oh, how she wanted to tell them everything, to pour it all out on paper, letting them know and feel that she was doing just fine. And to get back an answer from them assuring her that they were all well. She tried to imagine their first letter. It might tell her that Luke was almost a man now, that Ellie had herself a beau, that Clare was getting set up to go farming on his own, and that Arnie was busy working the plow for Pa. She wanted to hear that the apple trees were in blossom, and the ever-bubbling spring had just been cleaned for the summer cooling, that soft green lay on the land, and the school bell was ringing clearly in the crisp morning air.

Missie's eyes softened with her musings.

"Oh, Willie," she said, "I'd never even thought of such a wonder."

"An' I been thinkin'," Willie said cautiously, probably in case it was a dream that would never be realized. "Been thinkin'—not a reason in the world thet I can see, why yer folks couldn't jest hop thet train someday an' make a trip out here."

"Oh, Willie," Missie cried, "could they really? Could people—it's not just for cows?"

Willie laughed. "'Course not. At the meetin' they said they 'spect lots of folks will be comin' out by train. Special car jest for folks to ride in—maybe even two cars iffen they be needin' 'em. Yer folks could come right on out, an' we could meet 'em at the station."

Missie caught hold of his sleeve. "It's too much—too much all at once. I feel I could simply burst if it doesn't stop."

"Don't ya go bustin'," Willie teased, pulling her to him. "We still got no doctor—an' I need ya. Who else is gonna look after Nathan an' me, an' git thet there house lookin' like a home 'stead of an empty, bare shell?" He chuckled as he held her close.

Missie was content to rest quietly in his arms.

"Speakin' of houses," Willie said against her hair, "iffen it's gonna be ready fer yer folks, I'd best git back to buildin' it. I decided today to send twenty or thirty steers along on thet cattle drive. No use doin' a thing by half measures. Soon as Scottie gits back with the money, I'll take one of the boys an' head fer Tettsford. An' this time, I'm takin' you, too, Missie. Iffen I don't git you away from this all-male company, you'll be losing all yer feminine charms!" But his eyes told her he didn't think that was likely.

Missie laughed, then retorted primly, "Why, yes, I believe I will be able to join you on your trip to Tettsford." But her dancing eyes gave her away, and she laughed again for sheer joy.

"We can git our winter supplies at the same time," Willie added.

"I need more preserving jars," Missie said. "Mercy! I planted more garden than either Cookie or I know what to do with."

Willie chuckled and released her.

"You be thinkin' on yer list," he said. "We'll be doin' our best to be fillin' it." He picked up his tools and started off for the new house. As he went he whistled, and the sound of it was pleasant to Missie's ears.

Around the corner of the cook shack limped Cookie, and close behind him trailed young Nathan, followed by his ever-present guardian, big Max.

Nathan chattered away and Cookie grunted in response. The dog was content to be the silent partner, giving an occasional wag of his tail.

Missie turned back to the little sod house. It was time to build a fire and begin preparing the evening meal. As she walked, she mentally composed her first letter home.

Dear Mama and Pa, she'd write.

God truly has kept His promise of Isaiah 41:10, just as you said He would. You should see our Nathan. He's about the greatest boy that ever was. He's quick, too, in learning and doing. You'd be real proud of your grandson. I think his nose and chin are like Willie's, but he has your eyes, Pa.

Truth is, we're expecting another baby. Not for several months yet, but we're excited about it. We haven't talked yet about what we'll do for the birthing and all, but maybe by then we'll have other folks around, and I won't have to go way back to Tettsford Junction. I pray that might be so.

Willie is building a stone house—our real house. The one that we've been living in, temporarily, is kind of small. It's been just fine, though, but now we're getting all set to move into the new one. We want to be in before winter comes again.

I have a nice big garden. It grows very well down by the spring. The soil is rich and easy to water there. I scarcely have to coax it along at all. Cookie, the cook, uses it for the ranch hands, as well.

I have chickens, too. This spring they gave us eighteen chicks, and we only lost two. I get seven or eight eggs a day. We're going to have chicken for Christmas dinner this year!

And we have neighbors! Maria is the closest one to the south. She is a very good friend, and we have enjoyed prayer times together. Soon Melinda, a friend from the wagon train, will live to the north of us. You remember our Henry, the driver that you found for us, Pa? Well, he met Melinda on the trip out here, and as soon as he finishes his house, they will be married. I can hardly wait.

We have a real good ranch foreman, Scottie, and several men who work the spread. There is Cookie—I mentioned him before—who is Nathan's favorite—mine, too; and Lane, Smith, Clem, Sandy, and two new ones whom I still don't know very well. The new ones haven't yet come to our Sunday Bible reading, but we're still praying. Their names are Jake and Walt. Of course they all have last names, too, except Smith, but we hardly ever use them here. Pray for all of them. Lane has become a real believer, but he takes a lot of ribbing from Smith. It would really help him if Jake and Walt broke from Smith and started coming on Sunday, too. Especially pray for Smith. He really needs God to thaw out his heart.

Missie pushed the kettle onto the heat and went outside for a new supply of chips. Her eyes traveled over the miles of hills.

They were not just distant barren knolls now, but separate, individual, each with its own characteristics. She remembered the coyote that appeared on that closest one. She had gazed at the one to the northeast when she looked for Willie's returning team. On the far ones she often saw the cattle feeding. The ones close by were covered with beautiful spring flowers. She'd transplanted some of them around the soddy door and watered them faithfully with her dishwater, almost always remembering Mrs. Taylorson's rule number four: All water must be used *at least twice.*

She turned her eyes toward the west. Even though she could not see them from her valley, her memory brought to mind the mountains—shadowy, misty, and golden by turn. "Like a woman," Willie teased, "always changin' in mood and appearance."

She turned back to the hills. How pretty they looked. In the distance were dots she knew were Willie's grazing cattle. A faster-moving black figure appeared for a moment and then disappeared over a rise—one of the hands checking on the herd. Another cowboy rode into the yard down by the corrals. Missie heard the thud of the hoofbeats and saw little smoky swirls of dust. She had missed her ride that morning. She would be sure to take Nathan out on the morrow. The sting of the wind on her face and the smell of sage in the air always awakened her and sent her home, eager to begin her day of scrubbing clothes or canning vegetables.

You know, her letter would go on, *how Willie boasted of his land when he came back? Well, it's even prettier than that. I didn't see it that way at first, but I love it now. The air is so crisp and clean, you can almost serve it on a platter. And the distant mountains change their dress as regularly as a high-fashion city lady.*

Missie filled her pail, hoisted it up and started for the sod dwelling.

Willie brought wonderful news today, her mental letter continued. *He says the railroad, which is coming soon, will not only haul out cattle but will bring people, as well. He says that you'll be able to come right on out here for a visit. Can you imagine that? I could hardly believe it at first, and now I can hardly wait. I never dreamed when I left back east that I'd ever be able to show you my home.*

Missie's eyes filled with unbidden tears. "My home," she said softly, realizing she had never said the words about this place before. "My home! It truly is! I don't feel the awful tug back east anymore. This is truly *my home*—mine and Willie's." Joy and pride filled her heart.

I can hardly wait to show them. Her thoughts tumbled over one another. *They'll love it. It's so beautiful—the mountains, the hills, the spring—I wonder if an apple tree would grow down by the spring. I could have Pa bring out some cuttings—it wouldn't hurt any to try.*

Missie turned back to the temporary soddy that had been her home for two whole years.

"You know," she said aloud as she paused in front of the door, "I'll almost miss you, my little first home with Willie. I think I'll ask him to leave you sitting right here. You can be my quiet place, and I can come here sometimes and think and remember—the Christmas dinners when we crammed in here all together, Cookie sitting there on that stool nursing Nathan back to us, the planning that Willie did at that little table, the dreams, the tears, the fears that we've shared here. I've done a whole lot of growing since I entered this door—and there's still more to do, I reckon."

Missie looked about her. What else would she tell Mama and Pa? Maybe very little more. Maybe it was best for them to come and see for themselves. It was hard to put hopes and dreams on sheets of paper. Dreams of a church and a school for Nathan and his brothers and sisters. Dreams of white curtains and a sunlit sewing room. Dreams of Willie with a herd the size he had always planned. Dreams of neighbors and friends, laughter and shared recipes. Shared prayer times.

It would be hard to put her dreams down in neat rows of writing. It would be so much better when she could open her door and her arms to her mama and pa and say, "Welcome! Welcome to my home. There's love here. Love that started growing way back on the farm and traveled all the way here with us, growing and strengthening every mile of the way. *God's* love—just as He promised. *Your* love, for us as your children. And *our* love for one another and for our son. Love! That's what makes a home. So, welcome, Mama and Pa. Welcome to our love-filled home."

Children's Books by Janette Oke

www.janetteoke.com

PICTURE BOOKS
(for all ages)

I Wonder... Did Jesus Have a Pet Lamb?

JANETTE OKE'S ANIMAL FRIENDS
(full-color, for young readers)

Spunky's Diary
The Prodigal Cat
This Little Pig
New Kid in Town
Who's New at the Zoo?